The Medicine Men

Men of medicine were supposed to be concerned with the welfare of *all* their patients,
even in racist South Africa. So Dr Neal Potter,
starting his psychiatry training, believed. Until
he came across a suicide in a black patient
which his superiors seemed much too keen to
keep low-key. His curiosity aroused, he un-
covers other suspicious practices that lead him
to find irregularities on the part of the white
doctors at Durban's Wellington Hospital and
on the part of a Zulu witch doctor. But were
these irregularities accidents, or were the medicine men, black and white, not what they
seemed?

The Medicine Men is about the horrors that
lie just beneath the surface of ordinary medical
practice. Uncovering the truth takes Potter
from his hospital duties to black townships and
remote asylums on a chase that threatens both
his survival and his sanity. Piecing the puzzle
together requires all his detective skills and
medical technology. But they are not enough
to prepare him for the surprise awaiting him
—a surprise that will endanger his life.

LAWRIE REZNEK

The Medicine Men

COLLINS, 8 GRAFTON STREET, LONDON W1

William Collins Sons & Co. Ltd
London · Glasgow · Sydney · Auckland
Toronto · Johannesburg

This is a work of fiction. The City of Durban of
course exists, but there is no Wellington Hospital and
no Umzimkulu Rehabilitation Unit, nor do any of their
staffs and patients exist outside the author's imagination.

First published 1990
© Lawrie Reznek 1990

British Library Cataloguing in Publication Data

Reznek, Lawrie
    The medicine men.—(Crime Club)
    I. Title
    823 [F]

ISBN 0 00 232282 X

Photoset in Linotron Baskerville by
Rowland Phototypesetting Ltd
Bury St Edmunds, Suffolk
Printed in Great Britain by
William Collins Sons & Co. Ltd, Glasgow

To my father-in-law
Arthur,
with thanks

CHAPTER 1

There was a brief moment when Gloria Tembu knew she was going mad.

The woman in the next bed was moving. No. She was growing, slowly distorting, into some monstrous shape. The first thing to change was her face, her nose growing into a grotesque snout, her mouth widening and snarling with bared fangs, her eyes becoming cold and bloodshot. Next her arms metamorphosed. Hairs sprang out of every pore, claws from every nail. Then the limbs began to elongate, growing longer and longer, reaching out towards her.

Gloria Tembu closed her eyes, but it did not help. The monster was still there.

Something was obviously wrong. Closing your eyes is supposed to shut out the world. Unless you are seeing things. This moment of insight flickered and died all too soon, leaving Gloria to contend with the monster.

Gloria opened her eyes only to see the creature growing ever bigger, ever more terrifying, now towering over her, its saliva dripping from its jaws on to her face. She wanted to scream, but her voice had gone.

Then the creature reached out, not for her, but for the baby in the adjacent cot, its claws sinking into the baby's soft and shiny skin. Craning its long serpentine neck forward, it sank its teeth into the infant, the skull cracking audibly, saliva mixing with blood and brain. The creature tugged and pulled violently, the head coming away easily in its jaws.

A creature that eats infants. It was the tokolosh!

Gloria bolted out of bed, rediscovering her muscles, and made a run for it down the corridor between the beds. She hoped the tokolosh would prefer the newborns.

As she swung round the corner, she collided with the

night nurse and would have flattened her had it not been for the drugs trolley behind them.

'Gloria, what is the matter?' the sister managed as she straightened her skewed nursing cap.

'Just you stay away from me, you white devil! Don't think I am fooled! You are with the tokolosh! Now let me go!'

With that, she shoved the sister aside and sprinted for the archway with the sign 'Toilets' hanging over it.

Once inside, she was at a loss what to do. She could bolt herself into one of the cubicles, but that would be only a temporary solution. There was no other exit, there was no place to hide either. She was trapped.

It was then that she realized she could fly. It was then that she looked for a window through which to make good her escape.

When a body falls fifteen storeys on to concrete, it is not a pretty sight.

Dr Neal Potter swallowed hard. His training was no preparation for such a gruesome assault on the senses.

An obese black woman, probably around thirty (but it was hard to tell) dressed in a hospital-issue tunic. Her skull had taken the brunt of the impact, splitting open like a ripe watermelon, spraying its grey pips around her head.

'Details, details,' Neal reminded himself as he wiped the sweat from his forehead.

He forced his eyes down from what remained of the head to the torso. It, too, had been burst open by the impact, spilling its coils into the gutter.

A slaughtered heifer with offal on view, steaming and foul-smelling.

'Yugh! Enough to make you sick, hey?'

Neal turned to see a male nurse staring with unseemly interest at the remains. But he welcomed this distraction.

'Ja. But don't just stand there, man. Get a sheet or something.'

The nurse wrenched his eyes away and scuttled back towards the grey building that was Wellington Hospital.

Neal watched him disappear before turning to gaze through the sea mist at the lights of Durban harbour and the Indian Ocean beyond. For a moment he forgot the body, the stench, the one o'clock phone call that had yanked him out of a dreamworld.

'Trouble on Post-Natal Ward B,' the sister had said. And she hadn't been kidding.

Hell, Neal thought. What a start.

There was nothing like being thrown in at the deep end. It had been his first day as a psychiatric registrar, and they had put him straight on night duty. This made him responsible for all psychiatric referrals from GPs, for every crazy person wandering in off the street, for all ward emergencies—and for this.

He drove his hands into his jacket pockets, hunching his broad shoulders. He was tall and lean, his jacket concealing a swimmer's build fashioned by hours in the Durban surf. As he looked again at the remains, his youthful features tensed, burying his brown eyes behind two slits, with his black brows meeting in a line of concentration.

He was not squeamish, but this was something else.

The nurse returned with the sheet, taking one last long look before doing the decent thing.

Neal watched the blood soak into the white sheet, spread, and finally coalesce into a distorted human form.

The superintendent would have to be informed. The police, too. Statements given. It was going to be a long night.

'Stay here, will you?' Neal asked. 'I'm going to get the police.'

The nurse nodded, his gaze not moving from the shrouded corpse.

'Christ, Nurse! You ever consider the undertaking business?'

'Huh?'

'Forget it,' Neal muttered, and made his way up to the solitary open window fifteen storeys above.

He found the ward sister walking up and down in the

nursing office, wringing her trembling hands. She was a frail woman in her sixties, about to retire, but too proud to throw in the towel early. The years of nursing had taken their toll, and her thin frame was matched by a fragile disposition.

'If I've told them once, I've told them a hundred times. Those unguarded windows are simply unsafe. It gives the patients vertigo. Or strange ideas. But did they listen to me? Does a brick wall have ears?'

She stopped in front of Neal and lifted her hands in the air, palms upturned, as if she was waiting for manna.

'Listen, Sister. It's not your fault.'

'Of course it's not my fault. I kept telling them. And this is not the first time, you know. It probably won't be the last time either, unless they do something.'

Neal gently returned her arms to their sides and guided the elderly sister back to the chair by the observation window. Her wrists were as thin as her defences. Then he perched on the desk and picked up the phone.

'We will have to give a statement to the police. It's routine, and nothing to worry about. Now you just collect your thoughts and tell me what happened.'

The sister nodded. She did not like it, but rules were rules. And she was not about to depart from the letter at such a late stage of her career. While her trembling hands smoothed the folds in her uniform, she tried to think. There was just one small problem. Did she really know what had happened?

'Switch, get me the Harbour Police Station, will you? Ja. I'll hold.'

Neal turned to the nurse. 'Now, what happened?'

'Dr Potter . . .' The sister read the crooked name badge on Neal's jacket. 'Nothing happened . . .'

'Nothing? And a patient lies dead on the pavement?'

'I know, but . . .'

'You called me, didn't you?' Neal tried to be as gentle as possible, but he hadn't had enough sleep. 'You asked for the duty psychiatrist. You said there was trouble on Post-Natal

Ward B. Now just what do you mean, nothing happened? You saying you just phoned me up on a hunch?'

'Well . . . yes. It was the look in her eyes.'

Neal was about to lose his patience when he was interrupted.

'*Die polisie hier,*' the phone crackled.

'Hallo. Duty doctor from Wellington Hospital here. I have to report a probable suicide. She fell fifteen storeys. Can you come?'

'May I ask whether the superintendent has been informed?'

'No.'

'Well, do so first, Doctor.'

'Hold on a second,' Neal queried. 'Isn't it a bit silly for me to ring off now and have to phone a minute later?'

'Look, Doctor, don't get smart with me. Just contact the superintendent. Then we can talk.'

The phone went dead.

Neal pursed his lips. This was not the way his first night on call should be going. He dialled the switchboard again. Time to wake up Dr Michael Isaacs.

'Sure. I'll take the responsibility of waking him. And I'll hold.'

He did not have to wait long. Soon a slurred voice was grunting an acknowledgement at the other end.

'Dr Isaacs, it's Dr Potter here. I have a probable suicide on Post-Natal Ward B—'

'I'm on my way,' Isaacs interrupted.

Neal shrugged his shoulders as he replaced the receiver.

'The superintendent's a bit keen, isn't he?' he thought aloud.

'All show, doctor. He's up here like a shot, but what does he do?'

'Hmm. Let's see where she jumped, Sister. That will give you some more time to figure out a story.'

They walked out of the nursing office into the ward where a single night-light silhouetted the shifting shapes of patients trying to snatch some well-earned sleep. The blades of a single fan glinted as they propelled hot air downwards from the ceiling. It was summer in Africa and it was hot.

They found the place easily enough. Underneath the open window there was a chair balancing precariously on top of the toilet seat. The last step before oblivion. They stood in the toilet cubicle without speaking as if in a silent memorial.

After a while Neal took her arm and led her back into the ward. Once in the office, the sister took a deep breath and began.

'Her name was Gloria Tembu, Dr Potter.'

'When was she admitted here?'

'Yesterday morning, Doctor, after her baby had been stillborn. I saw it in the sluice room . . .'

Neal nodded and waited for the nurse to continue.

'She had been upset all afternoon, shrieking and wailing like it was the end of the world. When I came on duty at eight o'clock she was in bed, restless as ever. I offered her some night sedation, but she just stared through me as if I wasn't there.'

The sister shook her head.

'Then an hour ago she fled in a frenzy to the toilet, like she had the devil in her, saying something about me being in league with the tokolosh! That's when I called you. You see, it was the look . . .'

Just then two men strode into the ward perfectly in step like some small army unit. The first to enter was the superintendent, Dr Michael Isaacs. He was short and plump, with a rounded greasy face that glistened in the dim light. His full cheeks left only narrow slits for his eyes which peered through at Neal with irritation.

The second was an imposing man, large, craggy and solid. He looked archetypally Afrikaans, with short cropped brown hair, a square face, thin lips, and a white goatlike beard lending a pompous finishing touch. Neal recognized him immediately as Professor Jan Brandsma, head of Obstetrics and Gynæcology. In the last few months Neal had assisted him in his private operating to earn some extra cash.

'I'm sorry to have got you up at this hour,' Neal began. 'But the police suggested I contact you first.'

'I've told you housemen a hundred times,' Isaacs shouted. 'If there is a suicide on the Obstetric wards—any ward— I am to be contacted first. Not so?'

'I'm one of the new psychiatry registrars that started today,' Neal explained. 'We had no such instructions.'

'Then where is the houseman?' Isaacs turned to the nurse.

'Doctor, I thought I should contact the psychiatry registrar direct. She was looking all strange . . .' The sister trailed off, withering under the superintendent's glare.

Then Isaacs turned to Neal, forcing a smile. 'A question of ignorance, then. I'll let it pass. But to repeat, any suicide must be reported to me, do you hear, before the police are informed. I know the right channels, and you know what the police are like. They want things done by the book . . .'

There was an awkward pause. Neal said nothing.

Then Brandsma asked in his thick Afrikaans accent what had happened. He listened in silence as Neal told what he knew.

'A clear case of suicide, wouldn't you say?' he said as he turned to Isaacs. 'Upset about the stillbirth.'

'Ja. No need for you to hang around, Dr Potter. We will sort things out.'

'You don't want me to wait to make a police statement?' Neal offered.

'No need for the police at this stage,' Isaacs replied.

'Should I order a district surgeon's post-mortem?'

'I'll take care of that,' Brandsma returned. 'Produce a statement for the police by the morning, and send it to me via the internal mail. You see, she is, or was, my patient.'

Neal hesitated. 'Isn't it standard practice to have the police involved at this stage?'

Isaacs shifted his weight. 'Not standard practice, Potter. No. Obviously they have to be involved, but any time within twenty-four hours will do.'

'Right, then.' Neal shrugged. 'I'll be off. You'll find one of the nurses with the body. On the concrete.'

Then he left, still surprised that superintendents and professors were prepared to do the donkey work. He wasn't about to complain.

But it did make him wonder.

CHAPTER 2

Neal was fooled by their appearance. They looked like ordinary rows of office cabinets, grey, metallic, ceiling-to-floor. Until they were opened. He found out the hard way.

'Her notes are in cabinet twenty-four,' the pathologist said casually. 'Can you pull them for me?'

Neal walked over to cabinet 24 and gave it a confident yank. He didn't find any clinical notes. Instead, looking up at him and grinning stupidly was one very dead woman.

'Jesus!' he gasped, his body jolting backwards.

The pathologist guffawed, slapping him on the back. 'Should've seen your face. Man, it was paler than the corpse's!'

With that, he turned and led the way out of the office. 'Come on!' he called. 'I'm doing her now.'

Neal unglued himself and followed the pathologist's stocky figure to the morgue.

'Necrophilic sense of humour you guys have.' Neal managed a grin.

'Already a psychiatrist, huh? Diagnosing perversions wherever he goes,' the pathologist sang-spoke.

Neal raised his eyebrows in resignation. Then they were in the morgue. It was built like an operating theatre— windowless, tiled in clinical white, with suspended surgical lights. Except for the fact that there were a number of tables. And for the fact that the bodies on the tables were dead.

'Here she is.' The pathologist pulled the plastic green sheet off the body with the flourish of a matador.

Neal braced himself.

'Must have had a splitting headache,' the pathologist quipped.

He pulled down the metal arm from the ceiling and was soon cutting through the sternum to the sound of a high-pitched whine. There was no need to open the abdominal cavity—nature had already performed an amateurish job.

He was a good pathologist, and was not shy about it either. Work was something that transformed him, his short stature no longer obvious as he stood over the body, his awkward movements becoming graceful, his stubby fingers assuming a delicate touch as he teased the secrets from the body. This was his home, his castle. While he worked, he spoke into the dictaphone in his top pocket.

'In summary, a twenty-eight-year-old Zulu female with fractured skull, broken neck, and ruptured abdomen. Skin on back shows markings from concrete pavement. Hypertrophy of uterus shows recent pregnancy. No other pathology. Cause of death: fall from some height,' he ended.

Then he turned to face Neal.

'Now, then. What were these questions you wanted to ask?'

Neal cleared his throat. 'How come this is not being done by the district surgeon?'

'Simple. In uncontroversial cases the police are quite happy to appoint a member of the hospital staff to perform the post-mortem. Nothing unusual about that. Next?'

'Well, I was rather hoping the post-mortem could tell us something.'

'Like?'

'Whether there is any evidence of foul play. You see, Dr Isaacs and Professor Brandsma turned up pretty promptly last night, and both seemed awfully keen to sort things out on their own, like there was something to cover up.'

'I can't see any evidence of foul play, detective. This looks pretty obviously like suicide.'

'Then tell me why they seemed twitched by it all?'

'Sure.' The pathologist led the way out of the morgue,

wiping his hands on his already bloodied apron. 'This is the fifth suicide from that ward in the last year.'

There was a loud knock at the door, not the sort of knock made by an inferior.

'Come in,' called Isaacs, rubbing the sleep from his inflamed eyes.

Isaacs was still recovering from the busy night and the squabble with his wife that had followed in the morning. Whine, whine, whine, like a garden of Christmas beetles in the mating season. She was always like that when a phone call disturbed their sleep. At times like that he knew he should have remained a bachelor.

He finished rubbing his eyes and looked up. 'Jan! Take a seat.'

Brandsma lowered himself warily into the leather chair. He said nothing.

Finally Isaacs coughed. 'You know I can't go on doing this.'

'Doing what?'

'Goddamnit, man! You know very well what. Covering for you, that's what. Keeping the police off your back. Jesus, man, I can't do it forever.'

'OK, man. I really appreciate what you are doing, and I know you are sticking your neck out and all that. But the fewer people snooping around . . .'

Isaacs simmered down.

'Ja, I know. That was why I said I would get involved in the first place. But I don't like these deaths, man. Can't we do something about that?'

Brandsma nodded. 'We can bar up the windows, maybe get some better trained staff. But how can we do this without arousing suspicion?'

'Hmm.'

The two men sat in silence in Isaac's subterranean office. It was clearly an administrator's den, peopled with filing cabinets on both sides and paperwork stacked in two trays on the large oak desk. There was no hint anywhere that

Isaacs was a qualified doctor. That was the way he wanted it.

Isaacs changed the subject. 'Do you think the registrar suspects anything?'

'I don't think so. But we can't take any chances. We'll have to keep a close eye on him.'

CHAPTER 3

Selina Zondi held on to her grandfather as she was racked by another wave of pain.

Cedric Zondi had to use all his wiry strength to support her. In the end he was thankful that other people in the queue came to his aid. For Selina was not a small woman, and he was not a young warrior any more.

Almost as soon as the pain had come, it passed off, enabling Selina to stand on her own. That gave the old man a chance to search once more for the tell-tale spiral of dust. But the horizon was clear. The bus for Wellington Hospital was late, as usual.

Although the years had bent him, rounded his shoulders, and stiffened his joints, they had not cowed him. Life had been hard, as it was for most blacks in South Africa, but he was not one to give up easily, and this showed itself in his grimly set jaw and his steady gaze. He had the face of someone who had seen it all, tufts of white beard punctuating his leathery face, partly obscuring the deep furrows that time had ploughed into his skin.

'Cedric Zondi!'

The words were spoken as a challenge, making the old man spin round.

. It was the witch doctor, dressed in all his finery, his leopardskin tunic shining in the sun, his silver bangles jangling on his ankles as he strode up to them, his necklace of magical charms rattling on his chest as he breathed.

He had an aristocratic face, high cheekbones, a strong

chin, and narrowly set eyes. There was the height to go with it, and he used it to good effect, now towering over the wizened old man. A hundred years ago he might have been a Zulu chief. Now his power was considerably less, but this made him more dangerous. He was not a man to be crossed.

'*Sabonna*, Joseph Nongoma,' Zondi answered coldly.

'I have warned you before, old man, about seeking the white man's medicine.'

Cedric nodded.

'I warned you when you took young Gordon to the white man's clinic for his vaccinations,' Nongoma continued remorselessly, casting a spell of silence over everyone at the bus station.

'And not long after there was an epidemic of the Battle Cry Cough.'

Cedric stared into the distance, seeing only the lifeless form of his grandson in his arms.

'And soon Gordon was dead.'

Nongoma paused to let the cruel words tear at the wizened man in front of him.

'And now you choose to reject my medicine for Selina, and send her to the white man's healing kraal instead. Have you not seen for yourself that the white man's medicine is poison?'

Cedric pulled his shoulders back. 'It is because your medicine has failed to help Selina that we are sending her to Wellington.'

'Failed! You will learn about the meaning of failure if you send Selina to the white man. I warn you, Zondi. I shall not forget this.'

His words were swallowed up and lost in a cloud of dust as the bus swept into the station. Suddenly unmesmerized, the crowd surged towards the door, almost knocking over the old man and his granddaughter.

Cedric was grateful for the interruption. He turned and pushed Selina towards the door. But before he could get very far, Nongoma grabbed his shoulder in a hawklike vice and spun him around.

'Do not forget that I warned you, old man. You will live to regret the white man's medicine.'

Nongoma's face was inches away, and the words were spat with venom.

Then he was gone.

The casualty house officer creaked his tall body erect and groaned. It looked like he was not going to get away early.

He had been trying to determine the nature of his last patient's heart murmur when the casualty sister had poked her head through the curtains and bellowed 'Emergency!' into his stethoscoped ears.

The house officer pursed his lips, gave himself a moment's grace, and looked across at the nurse.

'Sister, just what sort of emergency are we talking about, please?' he said testily, removing the stethoscope from his ears and flinging it around his neck like a scarf.

'Collapse!'

'Damn!'

There was no time to waste.

The sister led him to the cubicle at the end of medical casualty where she and a porter had dragged the collapsed Zondi woman. They jostled with the blank-faced patients milling in the corridors and the blue-overalled porters steering trolleys to and fro. When they reached the cubicle, they found their patient doubled over in the foetal position.

The casualty officer turned his medical gaze on the patient. From the way she was lying, it was obvious that she was suffering from abdominal pain.

'Looks like a surgical emergency,' he thought aloud. 'Still, I'd better cast an eye over her. Ask her what the matter is, Sister, will you?'

The cubicle was soon filled with the clicking sounds of the Zulu language, the nurse firing questions and Selina Zondi whispering replies. When the clicking was over, the nursing sister looked across the bed at the houseman.

'She says it's the tokolosh.'

'And that is the Zulu word for appendicitis, is it?'

'The tokolosh is the evil spirit Zulus believe is responsible for all their ills,' the sister replied sharply, declining to take the bait. She disliked sarcasm.

'And I suppose this tokolosh has invaded her abdomen?'

The houseman did not wait for her reply, roughly checking the rest of her vital signs. A torch flashed into her eyes revealed widely dilated but reactive pupils. A stethoscope on her chest revealed good air entry and a racing but normal heart. He abandoned measuring her blood pressure in exasperation because the cuff was not big enough to get around her obese arm.

Then he turned to her abdomen. He made the sister help him lift up the patient's soggy dress to expose her rolls of fat. Gently at first, then more searchingly, he probed her abdomen, concentrating on the tips of his fingers. At first his hand disappeared into the folds of fat, but it soon encountered a boardlike resistance.

'Peritonism! I bet it's a burst appendix.'

He straightened up, satisfied, hoping he could get away early after all.

'Whatever it is, it isn't a medical problem. Sister, bleep the surgical registrar. And quick!'

The surgical registrar was already in Casualty, looking at another referral, and was soon pulling the curtains aside and surveying his new case. He was a short, chubby man, but unlike the archetype, he was not jovial.

'Ja? So what does the casualty houseman think he's got for me here?' he asked severely.

'I think she has peritonism.'

'*Think?* Good God, man! If you only think someone has peritonism, then he hasn't. Where did you learn your surgery?'

The house officer did not answer. It had not been a question anyway, for the registrar was no longer looking at him. He was burrowing his way to the bedside to survey the patient.

Like a surgeon, he treated her as an abdomen with arms and legs and straight away began to prod Selina's exposed midriff. There had been no word of greeting. He continued exploring her abdomen for a long period of time while the houseman shuffled his feet nervously. Finally he straightened himself, turning sharply to face the junior doctor.

'I don't suppose you've done a vaginal?'

The house officer shook his head miserably.

'Well, you know what happens, don't you? If you don't put your finger in it, you'll put your foot in it,' the registrar continued crudely. 'Don't just stand there. Put on a glove.'

The houseman walked sheepishly to the metal trolley in search of a glove, grimacing at the registrar when his back was turned.

'Tell her what we're going to do, will you?' he addressed the casualty sister while he snapped on a pair of disposable rubber gloves. Then he proceeded to push the patient's huge thighs apart.

Selina Zondi cried out, shrinking back in horror. She made a frantic effort to kick the doctor away, but she was tired. And in pain.

It did not take the nursing sister long to pin Selina down. Then the house officer shouldered her tense knees apart and drove his finger into her most private space.

The vaginal examination was difficult because of all the fat. In order to reach the cervix, he had to lean forward and push. Then he felt it. A hard mass where the cervix should have been. He felt again.

'Oh Christ!' the houseman swore. 'She's in bloody labour!'

He was feeling the head of a baby.

CHAPTER 4

'What do you mean – they're not there?'

Neal combed his long fingers through his thick black hair and frowned. That sinking impotent feeling he usually felt when confronting bureaucracy was there again.

'I'm sorry man.' The coloured clerk in the records office shrugged his shoulders.

'Ja, don't say it. You just work here.'

'That's right, man. Be cool.'

Neal tried, but it was difficult. He had spent two days trying to understand his superiors' behaviour, trying to tell himself there was nothing untowards going on. Until he had become irritated at himself. Rationalizing away awkward facts was not one of his weaker points.

'Tell me what happens when a patient enters the hospital?'

'Well, that's easy. They go to admissions where they get a number, man. That's when they're computerized, if you see what I mean?'

The clerk grinned; he had nothing better to do.

'Right. So we ought to have Gloria Tembu on the computer?'

'Right on, man. And we do.' The clerk punched his finger at the visual display unit to emphasize the point.

'That's how we get her folder number?'

'Right again. 479326.'

'So there ought to be no trouble procuring her folder from the files?'

'Sorry, man. Like I told you. The folder is not there, grown legs, gone walkabout, know what I mean?'

Neal thought of something. 'Is there a tracer card?'

'Gone too, missing—'

'OK, OK,' Neal cut him short.

He would have to try another tack. 'Does the computer give you access to names if you put in a diagnosis?'

'How'd you mean?'

'If I want to find out all the people who have had, say, breast cancer, in the last year, can I do it?'

'No problem, man. What you say the diagnosis was?'

'Suicide.'

The clerk give Neal a knowing look as he sat himself down at the keyboard. In a few moments he had a list of names on the screen.

'How many female cases are there?'

'Five.'

'Can you get their notes for me?'

'No probs.'

The clerk pushed himself away from the counter, sailing off on his swivel chair towards the shelves. He moved around like a spider with two legs, digging his heels in and pulling the chair up and down the aisles, stopping only to finger the notes as he passed.

It didn't take long. Then he was back at the counter.

'Sorry, man. They're all gone, missing, AWOL. And not even a single tracer card.'

When Dr Jill Bates saw her latest admission, she cursed under her breath. The patient was another candidate for Professor Brandsma's obesity trial. She shrugged her shoulders with resignation and directed the porters to Delivery Room 05.

05 and 06 were reserved for Professor Brandsma's trial. For the last four years he had been investigating the complications associated with obesity in pregnancy and labour. Although this was an interest he shared with few of his colleagues, his word was law in the Obstetric Department. Vital resources had been shifted from bread and butter obstetrics to make room for his hobby-horse. Two sorely needed beds had been blocked.

Jill Bates nodded to the porters as they approached the entrance of 05 and watched as they swung the trolley into the windowless interior. Then she looked down at the frightened face of her new patient and smiled.

'*Sabonna*, Selina!' Jill read the name off the front of the folder.

Selina managed a smile. Jill's was the first kind face she had seen in the white man's hospital.

'*Sabonna*, Doctor,' she whispered.

The trolley jolted to a stop in the centre of the room. It was bare apart from the cardiotocograph on one side and the drugs cabinet on the other. In the wall were colour-coded sockets for oxygen, nitrous oxide, and a vacuum. The rest of the tiled room was featureless, sterile, and unwelcoming.

The black midwife, herself a candidate for Brandsma's trial if she ever relented and decided to have children, bustled into 05. She took in the scene at a glance, and pushed Jill aside to get to grips with the patient.

'*Moenie Dunza, Mommy! Moenie Dunza!*' she bellowed above the grunting noise Selina Zondi was now emitting.

Jill smiled at the fusion of three languages into one simple command: 'Don't push!' She watched as the midwife plugged the mask into the yellow wall socket marked 'Nitrous Oxide' and pressed it over the patient's nose and mouth.

'This is no time to take a history, Doctor. She's looks like she is in second stage!'

Jill moved into action, brushing her blonde hair off her fair skin, skin that belied an upbringing in the sun-wrinkling African highveld. Her large brown eyes flickered over the patient, observing the signs, her strikingly dark brows forming a line of concentration while her long graceful fingers steadily probed for information.

Though she would have been the first to agree that she was no beauty queen, Jill's face was animated by a lively intelligence and spirit. She had that sort of attractiveness generated by a warm and engaging personality. Hers was not a beauty that could be captured in any photograph.

She was also as skilled as she was attractive—it had been this that had persuaded Brandsma to take on his first female registrar. Soon she had sized up her latest clinical problem, and began searching for a vein, leaving the midwife to sling Selina's legs into stirrups and open the delivery pack.

It was then that Professor Brandsma entered with a group of students on a teaching round.

'What have we here, Bates?' he asked gruffly.

'Unbooked primigravida, Professor. Arrived in labour. Already in second stage.'

Jill looked up from her search, but Brandsma had already turned to one of his students.

'What is the biggest problem obesity presents for pregnancy?' he asked above the moans coming from the patient.

The student frowned and shook his head.

'Anyone else?'

No one volunteered.

'Making the diagnosis, of course. If someone weighs ninety kilograms, with rolls of fat like tyres, you have a hard time deciding whether she is female, let alone whether she is pregnant!'

Brandsma laughed, but the students did not join in. Then he instructed them to watch the delivery.

The head was already crowning, stretching the tough perineum and making Selina writhe and scream with the pain. She had now been instructed to push, but all her energy was coming out in a groan. At the foot of the trolley the midwife exhorted her to greater things, while Jill drove in the canula for the drip. A second nurse had been called in and was drawing up a drug in a syringe.

With a gush of liquor and blood, the head suddenly emerged, only to be seized by the midwife's over-eager hands and pulled downwards. The traction exerted was vigorous, almost violent, making one of the female students go suddenly pale and slide slowly down the wall on to the floor.

Then the shoulders came free with a loud popping sound. At this point, the associate nurse briefly swabbed the buttock and threw her syringe in like a dart.

It was time for another question. Brandsma turned to the group. 'What is the nurse giving the patient?'

No one knew. No one dared guess.

'Syntocinon. And does anyone know what that is?'

Again no one risked an answer. Brandsma turned to Jill, who was now standing to one side, the drip already running in.

'Its the synthetic form of Oxytocin, and we give it to make the uterus contract after delivery. This helps prevent uterine atony and consequent post-partum hæmorrhage.'

Jill smiled at the students. She enjoyed teaching, and she

knew she would make a good teacher. All she had to do was to survive her training with Brandsma.

'That is correct.' Brandsma nodded. 'With obese ladies we get obese babies. And with obese babies we get over-stretched uterine muscles. And with overstretched uterine muscles we get post-partum hæmorrhage.'

The midwife, with a final flourish, pulled out her one thousandth baby and announced to her audience that it was a boy. The unsuspecting newborn was then clapped on the back, suctioned, rubbed vigorously with a spiky towel, and dropped briefly on to the scales.

There was still the placenta to deliver before Selina could see her baby, so the midwife left him in the transparent plastic cot for a moment and let the female students cluster around and get broody. When the placenta was out, the midwife went round to present the new mother with her healthy nine-pounder.

Selina took one look at the baby and let out a terrified scream. She pushed her weakened body up on to her elbows, her eyes widening all the time with a mixture of horror and perplexity. Then she lunged at the startled midwife, scratching at her child.

The midwife was caught off guard, and the two large women toppled on to the floor, the baby sandwiched be-tween. The trolley, still attached to Selina's stirruped legs, crashed over on top of them. Then the drip-stand went over, shattering the flask of normal saline and ripping the IV line out of Selina's arm. Soon blood was gushing from her vein, anointing the midwife and the child.

When Selina began punching at the midwife and her child with a frenzy born of terror, the others in the room suddenly thawed and rushed over to help. The trolley was yanked off the struggling pair by some of the students, leaving Jill to tackle Selina. She managed to get an arm round the black woman's neck, while the nurse pinned down one of her flailing arms. Then the students rallied round and pushed Selina off the midwife.

It needed both nurses, Jill, and some of the students to

finally pin her down. When she recognized she was trapped, she began sobbing, unleashing a torrent of anguish.

'It is the tokolosh's child! It is the tokolosh's child!' she wailed in Zulu.

Only the midwife understood.

'What's this about the tokolosh?' Brandsma asked from a distance.

'I don't think the mother even knew she was pregnant, Professor,' the midwife explained. 'When she came into Casualty, she thought the evil spirit had possessed her. Now I think she believes the tokolosh has given her the child.'

'There you are.' Brandsma turned triumphantly to his students. 'The woman is so fat that even she didn't know she was pregnant!'

The students were ushered out. Brandsma had made his point and the lecture was over. They left Selina Zondi to cry.

CHAPTER 5

Cedric opened the door to let the tall shadow of the witch doctor fall across his threshold.

Joseph Nongoma was wearing his headdress of death. It was an awesome thing. Radiating from his head in one hundred and eighty degrees were spokes driven through hundreds of small monkey skulls like kebabs. And they were dripping with fresh blood.

Cedric Zondi shivered involuntarily. He prayed he was ready.

'I have come, old man.'

'I see you.'

'I have come, old man, not to take your life, but to try to help.'

'But why the dress?'

'Because you need it. Because your grandchild needs it. Because we need to fight death with death. For even now the white man's medicine seeps into her brain, driving her senses out, letting the tokolosh come in.'

'Hau!' Cedric groaned.

'I warned you, old man. You had your chance.'

'How do you know?'

'You still doubt me? Go tomorrow, old man, and ask the devil in the white coat. Ask him about the others, too.'

'The others?'

'Yes, old man. Selina is not the first.'

'Not the first?'

'Not the first to be claimed by the white man's evil medicine.'

'Are you the duty psych?'

Neal put down his fork before looking up. His reply was going to be abrupt and short. The day had already been too long. But that was before he saw who was inquiring.

The woman standing at his table was dressed in a white coat which served to accentuate rather than hide her slim and feminine figure. She had an open and attractive face, a smile already playing at the corners of her mouth. What held Neal's attention most of all were her eyes—big, warm, and brown; he could have willingly drowned in them. He stared hard till she blushed. But she did not look uncomfortable.

'Head-shrink, psychoanalyst, trick cyclist. Call me anything. I'm at your service.'

'Good.' She sat down at his table uninvited and smiled. 'I'm Jill. Jill Bates. I'm in obstetrics.' She extended a hand.

'Neal Potter,' Neal replied, bobbing briefly from his chair to shake her hand.

'What do you know about post-partum psychosis?'

Neal jumped. 'Not a great deal, as it turns out. I'm only a three-day-old psychiatrist, you know.'

Jill grinned again. 'I wanted to ask you about a patient who is worrying me. You see—'

'Sorry.' Neal touched her hands clasped together on the

table. 'Potter's Law: psychiatry and spaghetti don't mix. Tell me about yourself instead.'

Jill went red again. 'You're just dying to practise your newly-acquired interviewing skills on me, I can see,' she countered.

'No. Just interested.'

'OK. As long as we swap life stories.'

'Deal.'

'Well, I'm an obstetric registrar. And I present with a twenty-two-year history of hearing voices.'

'No kidding?' Neal grinned. 'When do you hear these voices.' He played at being concerned.

'Oh, it's only when people move their lips up and down.'

Neal laughed, putting down his fork. 'I'm getting nowhere, I can see. Let me think. You're twenty-two. Attractive. You're not the feminist type. But you feel that it is important to have a career, to be treated with respect, not to be owned. You're a little shy, but no wallflower, and can give as much as you get. Probably quite independent: you like company, but won't go along with the crowd just for the sake of it . . .'

'Sounds vague enough to be correct. Next you'll be telling me my sun sign!'

'Hmm. Let me see. Pisces?'

Jill looked surprised. 'How did you know?'

Neal winked, pointing to the partly concealed birthday card in her coat pocket. 'Pure masculine intuition.'

Jill laughed and shook her head while Neal gazed at her. He liked the way she moved, the way she threw her head back and laughed, the way her eyes shone with intelligence and humour. In fact, he liked everything about her. He hadn't been so attracted to anyone in a long time. And as he looked at her, he could sense that he was not the only one feeling that way.

The silence was strangely comfortable. They sat together, Neal finishing his meal, having to suck the wriggling tails into his mouth, while Jill sat watching, her eyes filled with amusement.

Finally Neal wiped his chin and broke the spell. 'Now. Was there something about post-partum psychosis?'

'Right.' Jill paused, struggling to orientate herself. 'What I really want to know is when it begins. Post-partum psychosis, I mean. And how you recognize it. You see, one of our patients seems quite disturbed, only she seemed disturbed before the delivery as well. And I was wondering whether we shouldn't keep an eye on her, or even give her something to calm her down?'

'As I said before, what I know about post-partum psychosis is dangerous. But I am prepared to go and assess her. As long as you'll come and hold my hand.'

Jill agreed, and they set off for the lifts together, walking in silence. The big metallic doors of the lift finally shuddered open and they walked in.

'Alone at last.' Neal broke the silence jocularly as the lift jarred upwards. He moved in front of her, preventing her from studying the progress of the lift floor by floor. 'I just wanted to warn you that I suffer from an Impulse Disorder. It's rare, and it only seems to happen when I meet beautiful women.'

'Oh?' Jill looked at him, her eyes dark and appealing.

'Yes. You see, I can't resist the impulses. They make me do this.'

He brushed her hair gently away from her face, bent over and kissed her. It was not a passionate, breathtaking embrace; it was more a gentle caress and did not last very long, but Jill reflexly swung her arm back and struck Neal on the cheek. He shot backwards, startled.

Jill immediately regretted it. It wasn't that she was not attracted to him. It was that no woman liked to be taken for granted.

Neal could have joked about his impulse disorder, but he had sobered. 'I'm sorry, really,' he offered.

The lift jolted to an unceremonious stop, and they were both grateful for something to do, walking quickly out into the obstetric ward in silence once again. It was a silence that was soon to be rudely shattered.

The shrill ululating sound Zulu women make before battle swept up the corridor and almost blasted them over.

They made their way quickly into the ward, absorbing the details of the commotion. A large black patient had overturned two beds to create a barricade in the corner. She was defending this territory from a group of terrified nurses by swinging a drip-stand over her head while ululating at the top of her lungs.

Jill seized Neal's arm. 'That's the woman! The one I was worried about.'

Neal nodded. Jill had been on the ball. Looking around for the blue uniform of the sister in charge, he spotted one lurking at a safe distance. It was the same one he had met on the night of the suicide.

'I'm pleased you are here, Doctor,' she blurted as she caught sight of them. 'And you too, Dr Bates. I was about to bleep you again. As you can see, she is quite disturbed.'

'What's been happening?'

'She's Selina Zondi, admitted this afternoon in labour. Only she had no idea she was even pregnant, and neither did the poor houseman! Since the birth she has rejected the baby, saying that it is the work of the tokolosh. On the ward she's been mute and withdrawn, hugging her knees and rocking back and forth. Until now, that is.'

'Thanks, Sister.'

'And, Doctor?'

'Yes?'

'She has the same look in her eye . . .'

'Same look?'

'. . . as the woman who threw herself out of the window.'

The splintering of a windowpane brought them back to the present. The woman had broken one of the windows. There was work to be done.

Suggesting to Jill that she hang back with the sister, Neal hurried to the end of the ward and asked the besieging nursing staff to back off for the moment. He didn't want to antagonize the patient.

Although Neal had only a few days' experience as a psychiatric registrar, he was acquiring important observational skills. What was immediately apparent was that the woman was highly aroused. She had a goitrous stare, her nostrils flared as she breathed, her skin rippled with goose bumps, and her neck pulsated rapidly with a tachycardia.

But the most striking thing was that she was having visual hallucinations. Periodically her eyes would dart about, following some imaginary object at which she would take a futile swing with the drip-stand.

'My first case of post-partum psychosis,' Neal thought aloud. He turned to the sister crouching nervously behind him.

'Sister, draw up 200 milligrams of chlorpromazine, will you?'

He disliked inflicting a stupor on his patients, but at least he had caught her before she took a dive. Chlorpromazine rather than concrete, any day.

The ward sister was soon running back with a syringe and an empty phial for Neal to check. Jill confirmed the contents for him.

'Right.' He nodded to a male nurse standing next to him. 'Next time she swings, try to pin her down. OK?

'OK.'

Neal stood back and waited. Then Selina Zondi took a swing.

The male nurse was ready. In a single leap he sprang over the bed and rammed into the patient. He caught her already off balance, and the two collapsed in a heap on the floor. Neal followed close on the nurse's heels.

Neal did not bother swabbing her thigh, or even pulling up her thin nightdress. He simply jabbed the syringe deep into her leg and, making sure he was not in an artery, he plunged the contents into the muscle. Then they struggled to hold her down.

Now it was a question of waiting. It would be a while before the drug would seep into her veins, travel to her brain, and slow the flood of nightmarish images.

*

Somewhere else in the hospital, someone was pacing up and down, locked in the unrelenting clasp of a moral dilemma.

From the outside he cut a pathetic figure—short, balding, and overweight, walking up and down his small office like a laboratory rat on a treadmill. He didn't seem to notice the fall of droplets of perspiration that trickled down his forehead and then off his eyebrows to stain his protruding abdomen.

Isaacs was not a happy man.

'I think I should just make a clean breast of it, go to the police, tell them everything. And throw myself on the mercy of the courts,' he thought aloud.

There was more pacing about.

'I'll have to resign, of course. And probably wouldn't get another job. I'd be penniless.'

More pacing.

'But he may know nothing. Maybe I should just sit tight. Weather it for a while. Cover my tracks. Work on an alibi . . .'

It seemed easier not to make an irrevocable decision, not to do anything, simply to wait.

He stopped briefly to peer out at the moon running away from the clouds across the sky. Then he continued pacing.

CHAPTER 6

They stood alone together in the corridor.

'I . . .'

'That . . .'

They spoke simultaneously. And then again.

'Sorry . . .'

'You were . . .'

Jill began to giggle. It was infectious, cathartic, sexy. And soon Neal was laughing, feeling the tension melt away.

'Gosh.' Jill spoke after a while. 'I haven't laughed like that in years.'

'Me too.'

A relaxed silence followed. The light from the wall lamp sparkled off Jill's eyes, communicated her warmth to Neal, and reflected his attraction back. They were still smiling, but as if the same thought suddenly occurred to them both, they grew more serious.

Jill reached up and touched Neal's cheek where she had struck him.

'I hope I haven't cured you of your Impulse Disorder . . .'

Neal didn't have to answer. He leaned over and kissed her. This time it was no gentle peck. The passion was there, and they both felt it, both acknowledged it, both surrendered to it.

Neal could feel himself being moved, and he almost marvelled at it. There was an ache that spread from somewhere deep inside his abdomen to his extremities, making them tingle. It was like fear, he thought, without the desire to run away.

His lips pressed hers, exploring their sensuous contours, thirsty to know their most intimate secrets. They were warm, wet, responsive. His breath was gone.

Their bodies embraced, Neal feeling out the shape of her feminine frame, her pelvis, her firm and pointed breasts through the barrier of her clothes, feeling himself become aroused.

'Beep, beep, beep,' the sharp and penetrating noise of Jill's bleep disrupted their embrace. They drew apart, Neal shrugging with amused resignation.

Jill's disappointment registered too. She nodded, opened her mouth to say something, thought otherwise, and shut it again.

'See you at the clinical meeting tomorrow,' Neal offered.

She nodded, and then was gone.

He must have stood immobile in the corridor for minutes. At least, that was the way it felt. Finally he had to ask himself what he was doing there. Then he remembered the blood samples.

Shaking his head to dislodge her image, he set off down

the corridor towards the Chemical Pathology Laboratory. The route lay in the bowels of the hospital. It was cold and dark, punctuated only by multi-coloured pipes filled with supplies of oxygen, nitrous oxide, and a vacuum, which snaked their way to the wards above.

Neal noticed none of this. He had begun thinking about the 600 milligrams of chlorpromazine they had given Selina Zondi. She had needed it.

It was amazing that she had tolerated such a large dose. A mere 50 milligrams would have flattened a normal person. In spite of the massive dose of chlorpromazine, the woman had remained highly disturbed, the flood of hallucinations almost unstoppable.

Perhaps she has DT's, Neal wondered. That would explain the visual hallucinations.

The difficulty was that he did not have a clear idea what post-partum psychosis looked like. Although he was a psychiatric registrar, and called upon to treat any imaginable disorder of the mind, he knew very little about many of them. It was a question of learning as he went along, though this was not something he was keen to tell his patients.

He resolved to read up other cases of post-partum psychosis. He disliked being ignorant about things. And then there was the behaviour of the superintendent and the professor to explain.

At the end of the corridor he turned right through a pair of swing doors signposted 'Chemical Pathology'. The reception area was bare apart from a blown-up photograph of a cell mitochondrion on one of the walls. Neal decided to ignore the bell and, lifting up the swing desk, walked straight into the laboratory in search of the duty technician.

Dr Mark McKenzie was poring over his notes when Neal strode into the room. He was the same age as Neal, but looked older because of his baldness. This was compensated in part by a rich red beard which hid most of his face. He had light blue eyes and a high forehead which was now wrinkled in thought.

He was doing research in molecular biology, but needed the overtime to pay for nappies, carrycots, and the paraphernalia that accompanied having a young son, so he had resigned himself to running the emergency chemical pathology laboratory every other night. A confessed night owl, he managed to do the theoretical aspects of his research when he wasn't running some laboratory test. There were not many of those moments, and when one arrived, he quickly lost himself in complex chemical equations.

It was in the midst of such equations that Neal found him. Only when he dropped the samples of blood noisily into the aluminium rack did McKenzie jerk his head up from his notes.

'Well, well. Hallo, Neal! What brings you here? I thought there were no psychiatric emergencies?' he joked.

Neal grinned. He knew the comment was only meant in good humour. They had been medical students together, and been nearly expelled together too.

They had come into conflict with the psychiatry professor over his Freudian dogmatics. The professor had been raised within the blinkers of Freud's vision of the human mind, and had become lost in a labyrinth of ego, superego, and id. Behaviourism had been dismissed with a single insult.

'Behaviourism is OK as a theory for rats. But we are not rats. Some of us, at least.'

The two friends had not been convinced. When the time came for them to do their psychiatry project, they had decided to test the Behaviourist theory. Not on rats, but on the professor.

The whole medical class had been roped in. They had been instructed to look incredibly bored and fidgety if the professor lectured without pacing about. On the other hand, they had been told to look fascinated and to take detailed notes only if he paced about the lecture room while he talked.

By the end of the twelve weeks' psychiatry training, the professor was literally running around the lecture theatre panting out his Freudian theories!

When the professor read the project, he 'blew his ego, lost his superego, and functioned only on his id', as Neal joked later. And it had been a very angry id at that. He had tried to get the students expelled, but thankfully there had been some sane members on the Medical Faculty. Since then the two had been best of friends.

'You're not up here to ask for a lab test, surely,' McKenzie continued. 'I thought head-shrinks didn't believe in physical causes?'

'Some of us have finally understood that the mind is occasionally influenced by what goes on in the brain. Although very, very occasionally, you understand,' Neal replied with mock sarcasm.

'OK, OK. I get the point. What can I do for you?'

'Mark, I need some emergency electrolytes, a full blood count, and some liver function tests . . .'

'Cross my palm with silver?'

Neal laughed. It was no secret why McKenzie was running the pathology laboratory at night.

'All right. Since it's you. It won't be too much of a hassle.'

'Mark, that would be great. I owe you. Listen. I mustn't stay, some of us doctors have to cure the sick, you know.'

He did not want to appear rude, but he was keen to look at the other cases referred from Post-natal.

'You mean psychiatrists can get cures these days?'

Neal grinned, giving his friend a dismissive wave. He left him to get on with the laboratory tests, his mind already on studying post-partum psychotics.

It would be easy to make up a list of such patients. All he needed to do was to gain access to the psychiatry professor's office and find the referral diary. Every request for a psychiatric consultation was sent to the professor's secretary, and she made a record of the referrals before distributing them among the registrars to see. In the record was a note of the patient's name and folder number, with the ward and department which had made the referral. So it would be a simple matter to collect the notes of all those patients referred from the post-natal wards. And as duty registrar, he had the master key.

It is easy to recognize which wards are the psychiatric ones. They are the ones with the self-conscious pictures of tranquil scenes and Snoopy posters, with the numerous Delicious Monsters jungling the corridors, with Zen Buddhist sayings on the walls, with the comfy chairs arranged in circles awaiting group therapy. Wellington Hospital was no exception.

Neal padded softly down the carpeted corridor avoiding the Delicious Monsters. The professor's office was half way down the corridor and he was soon inside. He felt like an intruder, and even looked furtively over his shoulder as he closed the door.

'Paranoia is an infectious disease,' he joked aloud. 'I was never like this until I started working in psychiatric wards!'

The office was spacious as if it was designed for treating claustrophobics. By the window was a large oak desk with two chairs on either side. Neal found the referral diary on the desk among the journals, letters, pens and paperweights.

He flopped into the professor's chair, opened the diary, pulled out his notebook, and ran his index finger down the column headed 'Ward'.

There weren't many referrals from the post-natal wards, and it was a month before he came across the first referral, Rachel Dlamini. He jotted down her name and folder number before continuing down the column. He had decided a year's cases would be enough to cure his ignorance. And to answer some awkward questions.

Neal worked quickly through the ward-referrals diary, soon collecting an impressive list of eighteen names. The wall clock chimed once, surprising him with how late it was. He didn't feel tired as his mind searched for solutions. He too was a night owl, his neurones only switching on as the sun went down, and he had long learned the futility of trying to go to sleep with a busy brain. Anyway, sleep was the last thing that he was thinking of at the moment.

Locking up after him, he hurried back to medical admissions. The admissions area had gone to sleep for the night, the benches empty except for an exhausted porter stretched out unconscious, the trolleys abandoned along the walls, and the curtains drawn to expose bare cubicles. Neal picked his way quietly towards reception.

In reception the night shift were playing cards. They were so absorbed in their play that they hardly looked up as Neal poked his head over the glass barrier.

Neal cleared his throat.

'Should we deal you in?' the admission officer mumbled without taking his eyes off his hand.

'Another time,' Neal joked. 'Right now I'll settle for the key to Obstetric Records. I need to retrieve some old obstetric notes.'

'Each to his own.' The friendly admission officer beamed back. Keeping his cards flush with his chest, he leaned over and handed Neal the key to Records, quickly returning to the game.

Neal made his way into the records room and walked up and down the rows of stacked pink folders. He soon had a pile of notes and staggered back with them to reception.

The admissions officer looked up from his game for the first time to wink at Neal. 'No more interruptions, please. Some of us have to work.'

'Sorry!'

Neal waved goodbye and let them get on with their game. He was anxious to get to work.

His office was a short walk away on the ground floor, a small, poky room that was bare apart from an old wooden desk and swivel chair. Its only virtue was that it was next to the registrar's coffee room. And the chair was comfortable.

He switched on his desk lamp and opened the first folder of the pile. It was Rachel Dlamini's. He was relieved to see that Jill's predecessor had done a thorough summary:

Patient	Rachel Dlamini
Date of Birth	7/5/65
Date of Admission	2/12/88
Date of Discharge	27/12/88
Consultant	Professor Brandsma
Registrar	Dr Fredericks

Present History

Rachel Dlamini is a 23-year-old unmarried primup who booked in at the ante-natal clinic on 12/11/88. She was unsure of her dates, and in view of her obesity an ultra-sound was done to stage the pregnancy. A singleton at 32 weeks was confirmed. The patient failed to attend any further ante-natal clinics, and finally presented to the hospital on 2/12/88 in established labour. She had begun having painful regular contractions two hours prior to admission.

Examination

The patient was in labour, 6 cm dilated, with the foetus in a cephalic lie. The patient was healthy apart from her obvious obesity.

Course and Management

Labour proceeded well with the cervix dilating at a rate of 1cm/hour. Analgesia consisted of intermittent nitrous oxide. Delivery was assisted by Wrigley's forceps when foetal distress was picked up on the cardiotocograph. Mother and child were discharged from Labour ward to Post-natal. 14 hours after delivery, the mother claimed that the staff had fed her baby to the worms and that the whole hospital was against her. She continued to see worms everywhere, and needed sedation with Chlorpromazine before being transferred to the Psychiatric wards. There she continued to hallucinate, elaborating a delusional system about whites feeding her and her baby to the worms. A diagnosis of Post-partum Psychosis was made, and the patient sedated with Chlorpromazine 100 mg QDS. She made little progress and was transferred to the Umzimkulu Rehabilitation Unit on 25/12/88.

Diagnosis
Post-partum psychosis
Prognosis
Poor, in view of her poor response to major tranquillizers.
May require up to 2 years' rehabilitation.

Neal leaned back in his chair and exhaled slowly. The
case seemed identical to the one he had just seen. He pressed
on.

The next folder was Miriam Umbuti's. The diagnosis
was the same, post-partum psychosis, so Neal went on to
read the summary. The pattern was compelling. If there
was ever a chance that he would get to bed that night, it
had now evaporated.

The next case was also similar. Too similar. In fact, that
was the puzzling thing. The cases had no clinical variety,
and there ought to have been. Nowhere in medicine do the
patients read the textbooks and present in identical and
classical fashion.

Just as he was settling down to figure it out, his bleep
interrupted his excited speculations. It was a call back to
Clinical Psychiatry. He hoped it would not be for long.

CHAPTER 7

Joseph Nongoma looked deeply into the eyes of the man in
front of him before finally casting the diagnostic dice.

It was obvious that the man's mind was disturbed, and
he let this intuition flow into the dice.

The dice scattered on the reed mat between the two men
sitting cross-legged in silence. The witch doctor averted his
gaze from his patient and studied the dice with a deep
concentration, leaving the patient to stare blindly through
him, seeing nothing.

'Look.' He spoke to the patient's brother standing behind
him, pointing with a skeletal finger at the pieces of the

pattern. 'The monkey's skull lies next to the poisonous root. This means that the poison is in the mind and not the body. There is nothing wrong with your brother's eyes, or his tongue. It is his mind that is not well.'

The still hot afternoon sun sank below the mud kraal which was the home and surgery of Joseph Nongoma, casting long shadows across the deserted market place. The stalls which an hour before had been full of impassioned bargaining were now abandoned, stripped bare of the day's produce. They would have to wait another day to be revitalized. The only actor on the stage was a stray dog who panted in the lengthening shadows, his eyes on the bones hanging around the witch doctor's neck.

Joseph still needed to find the cause. 'When did this begin?'

'Hau! Hau! It was a bad business,' the brother began. 'He is—was—a policeman. And you know what the comrades think of black policemen: they are the collaborators of the Pretoria regime, so they say. A month ago the comrades gathered around his house, intent on giving him and his family the "necklace" treatment.'

The medicine man raised his eyebrows inquiringly.

'You know. They put a rubber tyre round the neck and set it on fire.'

Nongoma nodded. The practice was becoming all too frequent in the townships.

'The comrades smoked the family out of the house and forced my brother to witness the necklacing of his own son. When they came to place the rubber tyre round his neck, the army forces arrived in Kaspar armoured vehicles. They had seen the smoke and soon dispersed the crowd. But by then my nephew was already beyond help. Ai! Ai! Ai!'

The man choked on his words, and Nongoma gave him time to recover.

'Almost immediately afterwards, he lost his sight,' the brother continued. 'And his voice.'

Nongoma returned his gaze to the diagnostic dice.

'Now look at this. The shark's tooth touches the eagle's

egg. This means that the spirits waiting to be this man's grandchildren are very angry that he did not save their would-be father. For now they will be forever denied the joy of earthly existence. It is these spirits that have come to torment him, robbing him of his tongue and sight.'

Nongoma had realized only recently that it was not only ancestral spirits that could cause torment.

'The explanation might be complex, but the prescription is simple,' the medicine man said encouragingly. 'If he, with your help of course, kills two lambs on two successive nights, offering them as an appeasement to the grandsons that he has denied a chance of life, I think they will be satisfied. He will then gradually recover his sight. And his speech.'

Nongoma pushed himself up from his cross-legged position.

'If you need any further help, just come to my kraal,' he ended the consultation.

The brother was greatly encouraged, confidence creeping back into his posture. He bent down to pick up the patient.

'Thank you very much. I . . . we will do exactly as you advise. Thank you again. We will not forget.'

After placing some money in the hollowed tree-stump at the entrance to the kraal, the brother helped his sick relative across the market place, fending off the stray dog who snapped irritatingly at their heels.

It was Nongoma's last patient, but he was not relieved. The day had only produced seven consultations, and he knew he could not survive on that, at least not in the manner to which he was accustomed.

Joseph Nongoma walked over to the stump to confirm his suspicions. There were some notes, but mostly coins. He counted only R26.50, not enough to keep his six wives and thirteen children, not enough to run his old green Cadillac, the envy of the township. The thought of selling it and losing his status filled him with anger, anger for the white clinic that had opened in Umfulosi Township a year ago to steal his patients, anger towards his own people for turning to

white medicine, anger at the white man's medicine that
brought only torment to his people.

It was time to see what news Sibiso Sithole had for him.
He slipped the money into a pouch sewn to the inside of his
leopardskin tunic and stalked across the open space towards
the white clinic.

The clinic was a prefabricated building standing on stilts
next to the main road, with rows of benches outside
shielded by a canvas canopy. It was deserted at this late
hour – the white doctors had flown back to their safe
suburbs.

Sibiso Sithole was seated on a wooden stool, resting his
back against the cool of the mud-packed walls of his kraal,
playing nervously with his pipe. He knew in his bones that
the medicine man would come, and he was not happy about
it. His brow was creased, and his dark eyes were not able
to rest anywhere.

It was not long before he spotted the tall lean silhouette
of Nongoma approaching him out of the dying sun and he
quickly shooed his womenfolk away.

'*Sabonna*, Sibiso.'

'*Sabonna*, Joseph.' Sithole returned the greeting, standing
up to welcome the doctor. 'How are you?'

'*Lungele*, thank you.'

Joseph looked preoccupied, not returning the question.
He seated himself next to Sithole, keeping his eyes on the
prefabricated building in the open square.

'Any more deliveries?' The medicine man came straight
to the point.

'How you know when to come, Joseph! Hau! I will never
know. But you are right. The truck with medical supplies
arrived today.'

'Then we have much work to do, my friend. Are you
prepared?'

'Ai! Ai! Ai! No good can come of this, Nongoma.'

Joseph's pent-up anger burst to the surface and he cut
Sithole short.

'What do you know about the spirit world, my friend?

Have you any idea what will befall us if we do not extract the poison from the white man's medicine?'

Sithole shook his head disconsolately.

'Take it from me, it has to be done. Otherwise you need not guess what evils will torment the households of Umfulosi, including yours.'

There was a threatening edge lurking in Nongoma's voice.

Sithole's misgivings were replaced by an impotent gloom and he resigned himself to helping the medicine man. He did not like it. Only the thought of his family made him settle in for the long wait for darkness.

Dusk came and went. The curfew bell rang and faded. Still the men waited, sitting motionless by the kraal, each locked into his own thoughts. Then the darkness came and grew ever deeper.

Finally Joseph broke the spell. 'It is time. Do you have the medicine?'

Sithole straightened his stiff body and retreated into the kraal. He returned with two large plastic bottles that sloshed with clear frothy fluid. Nongoma was now on his feet too, ready to direct operations. He nodded to his bearer to follow.

They stole stealthily round to the back of the white clinic, sticking close to the outskirts of the township like leeches. When they were lost to the view of the rest of the township, they moved up to the clinic itself, slipping under the stilts.

The route was familiar enough, for they had been there many times before. They soon found the trapdoor which they had cut painstakingly with a hacksaw blade, the trap-door into the white man's medicine stores.

It was heavier to lift than usual, indicating that the delivery had been a big one. When it was up, the medicine man stuck his head through the gap and poked around. He was looking for ampoules, the streptomycin for TB, the vaccines for tetanus, polio, and whooping-cough, the pethidine for pain, and many other injectable drugs. Nongoma knew that it would have been far too ambitious to have produced tablets to replace the white man's drugs. Replacing liquid drugs was easier.

He collected together the boxes of medicines and handed them back to his companion.

'We have to stop them, Sibiso. We have no choice.'

Sithole simply nodded his head with resignation. He knew what he had to do. Working quickly, he soon extracted all the phials of injectable drugs. Nongoma too was busy. Rummaging inside the medicine cupboard, he returned with some syringes and needles.

'Right, Sibiso, let us get to work.'

The light from the moon reflected off the ground, illuminating the two figures busy at work beneath the white man's clinic. It glinted off the fluid in the plastic bottles, the fluid they were withdrawing into syringes and injecting into the already emptied phials of the white man's drugs.

CHAPTER 8

Professor Jan Brandsma waved eighteen tracer cards under Isaacs's nose.

'He's got the bloody lot of them! We are going to have to do something . . .'

Isaacs groaned inwardly. It was not the way he had hoped the day would begin. First his wife had nagged him about his long hours, carrying on at him like a hyena in heat. Now this. Work was no longer a place of retreat. Then there was the fact that he still had to deal with delicate administrative difficulties.

'Now calm down, Jannie.' Isaacs took the tracer cards and fanned them out on his desk. A brief glance told him what he wanted to know.

'So he's interested in post-partum psychosis. So what does it mean?'

Brandsma shook his head angrily, struggled to come out with too many objections, and merely spluttered.

'OK,' Isaacs continued, gesturing towards a chair. 'So at most you are going to look a little negligent. He's not going to find anything more, surely?'

'He might mess the whole thing up, man. Can't you see that?'

Isaacs nodded. 'So what do you want to do? Scare him off? Show him an open fifteenth-floor window? Come on, Jannie, be sensible.'

The early morning sun streamed through the skylight and reflected off Brandsma's furrowed brow. For a while the two men were silent.

'Listen, Jannie. Let's just see what he does, OK? Nothing rash.'

Brandsma did not move.

Isaacs straightened, scooping up the tracer cards from the table and giving them back to Brandsma. He changed the subject.

'Don't forget the clinical meeting.'

'I won't.'

'We have to stick together on this one.'

'I know. We can't have these blacks reproducing like flies. It has to be stopped.'

When Jill walked through the hospital on her way to Obstetric Outpatients, the hospital was already bustling with activity.

It was Thursday, and that meant Jill spent the morning with her other boss, Dr John Peters, running the infertility clinic. He was a good teacher, and she was looking forward to it. Then there was the Clinical Presentation at twelve—Peters had said he had something special to present.

The Obstetric Outpatient Department was a little calmer. There were a number of depressed but hopeful couples huddled together on the waiting-room benches. Jill made her way to the Consultant's office. She knocked, waited for the 'Come in!' and walked into Dr Peters's room. He was on the phone.

'What do you mean, you are having to cut all departments? What other services have been cut?'

Jill didn't need a degree in psychology to work out her
boss was angry.

Peters was standing looking out of the window. He was
not a tall man but he made up for it with his solid frame.
A self-confessed fitness fanatic, he jogged every evening
along the beach, and consequently he did not look his
forty-two years. He was handsome, with light brown hair
that was greying at the temples, deep blue ey᠎᠎s, and a strong
masculine chin. In short, a man any woman would adore
to have as her gynæcologist.

Peters was one of those men who had no time for
authority, always speaking his mind and not suffering fools
gladly. As a result, he did not win many friends in high
places, although his manner made him popular with the
junior staff. Never before had so many students wished to
become obstetricians.

'So other cuts are under discussion? Is that it?' he bellowed
sarcastically. 'I suppose that next you'll tell me that your
job is under review?'

There was a pause.

'No? I thought as much.'

John Peters glanced in mock appeal to the heavens,
making Jill laugh.

'Listen. Some of us have a clinical job to do. Next time
you hold a meeting to review the allocation of resources, I
want to be informed. Is that clear?'

Without waiting for an answer, he slammed the receiver
down with disgust, shaking his head. Then he sank into his
chair, cursing under his breath.

'What was that all about?' Jill asked.

'That was Isaacs on the phone. Administration are cutting my Infertility Service. Apparently there was a policy
meeting last night, and Isaacs remembered to forget to
inform me about it.'

Jill thought of all the hopeful couples outside, and shuddered. 'What reason did he give?'

'He says the hospital budget is being cut. A government decision.' He shook his head. 'Of course they can't reduce the administrative jobs. These are essential, you know,' he continued with a heavy dose of sarcasm. 'So they say that they are having to cut all departments. It just happens that mine is the first and the only one so far to get the chop.'

'Sounds fishy.'

'I know. But don't you worry. I will be fighting it all the way.'

He stood up abruptly from his desk.

'Come. We have work to do. Even if they are going to cut my clinic, we still have patients to care for.'

Jill left the office, cursing the system she worked in. But as Peters had pointed out, she would do better by getting on with helping the patients already there. It was more fruitful than knocking her head against a brick wall.

She glanced at her appointments at Reception. Dr Peters liked her to see the new referrals, organize the basic investigations, and then discuss the cases with him afterwards. The diary was full, and she knew that if she did not get started straight away, she would not finish before the clinical meeting.

Time passed quickly. Jill lost herself in her work, enjoying the exercise of her medical faculties, grateful she could offer some help. The transformation of the couples as they passed through her office was most gratifying.

At five minutes to twelve, Peters popped his head round the corner and invited her to join him on the way to the clinical meeting.

'Dr Peters, I think you had better go ahead. I'll be a minute or two organizing these bloods.'

The consultant nodded, and disappeared. Jill hurriedly completed the forms for the hormone studies. She would have to race to get to the lecture theatre on time.

When she arrived, it was almost full. It was modelled on the old-style anatomy lecture theatres that sprang up in Italy at the time of da Vinci, tiers of ever-expanding circles telescoping upwards, providing interested doctors with a bird's eye view of dissections. N w the tiers were filled with junior doctors, consultants aid students rather than anatomists, busily talking among themselves.

Jill ignored the interested stares and looked around for Neal. She spotted him sitting near the aisle busily jotting in his notebook, and she was soon hurrying up the stairs. When she was two tiers away he looked up and grinned.

'Hi!' He stood up to let her through. When she was closer, he whispered: 'You look great!'

'Neal,' she warned. 'Take a hold of your Impulse Disorder, OK?'

Neal grinned. Before he could think of a witty reply, there was a rustle of papers at the podium, and they turned to see Peters preparing to present his case.

A hushed silence descended on the lecture theatre.

'The case I'm going to present to you today is the first case of successful *in vitro* fertilization carried out for an infertile black couple at Wellington Hospital,' Peters began. 'It is, I hope, the beginning of a service that we will be able to offer the increasing number of black patients who present to our clinic with problems of infertility.'

Peters paused to let his words sink in. He had aimed them directly at the hospital administrator who was dignifying the lecture with his presence. He was sitting conspicuously in the front row next to Professor Brandsma.

The case Peters presented was not extraordinary in medical terms. The couple had been trying to start a family for 10 years, but the wife had been unable to conceive because of blocked Fallopian tubes. Trying for so long was unusual for Zulu couples, for according to Zulu law, failure of the wife to conceive within two years was sufficient grounds for the husband to dissolve the marriage.

Illustrating his talk with a number of slides, Peters showed how he had harvested some of the wife's ova and fertilized them with the husband's sperm in a test-tube. He had then implanted the eggs into the wife's uterus, and she had fallen pregnant with twins on the first implantation, 36 weeks later giving birth to a healthy boy and girl.

'Perfect family planning.'

The audience laughed with approval as Peters closed his folder. Then he looked up.

'Any questions?'

'Would Dr Peters be so good as to tell us how much such a treatment costs the taxpayer?' Isaacs dived in without hesitation.

'I think the question is irrelevant, if you don't mind my saying so. This is a medical lecture, not an economic one.'

'My dear Dr Peters, don't be so naïve,' Isaacs persisted. 'Medicine was never separate from economics. Just take TB, or rheumatic fever. What do you think causes such conditions?' Isaacs's tone was condescending.

'Perhaps Dr Isaacs should ask any medical student that question. Aren't there things called bacteria?'

There was more laughter. The audience were enjoying themselves.

'You're wrong, Dr Peters. The cause is not the bacteria. These colonize everybody, but we don't all get the disease. No, Dr Peters, the cause is an economic one— poverty. It is poverty that weakens and makes some of us fall victim to such innocent bacteria. You obviously were brought up on the old-fashioned Germ Theory of disease.'

Dr Peters went red, and pointed his finger at the hospital administrator.

'Listen here, Dr Isaacs. You might profess to subscribe to the Poverty Theory of disease, but who was it who voted against the use of medical funds to improve black housing?'

There were gasps from the audience. Isaacs went white.

'Anyway,' Peters continued, 'you are not interested in having me tell you the cost of *in vitro* fertilization. You know it already. How else could you have calculated that the hospital could no longer afford to support the Black Infertility Service?'

Peters turned to the audience.

'Yes. I'm afraid that I have to tell you that the sort of work I have reported to you today is being curtailed. My funds are being reduced.'

There were murmurs from the audience. Disbelieving voices echoed the news.

'If the truth be known,' Isaacs responded. 'I think that it is outrageous that a hospital that struggles to deal with real life-threatening diseases like TB and rheumatic fever has to divert over R4000 for the luxury of satisfying the wishes of a couple who want children.'

'May I remind you that a course of adequate antibiotic treatment for TB costs well over R1000,' Peters rejoined smartly. He too had done his homework. 'Sending a patient back to his TB-infested home with his bottles of expensive drugs is tantamount to throwing the stuff down the drain. At least I get a cure. So don't throw the economic argument at me. It's likely to boomerang.'

Peters paused in mid-flight, but his raised finger indicated he wasn't finished.

'And how dare you consider infertility as not being a "real" disease? If you had the misfortune of being infertile, you would learn the meaning of the word "suffering". These couples are among the most unhappy I have ever come across in my career. And don't think that the illness is not life-threatening either: the incidence of suicide amongst infertile couples is close to three per cent.'

Isaacs spluttered, went red in the face, and bit his lip. Things were not going according to plan.

Then Brandsma stepped in.

'It seems to me that what Dr Peters has forgotten is the ecological dimension. It is appalling to me that you consider it appropriate to assist the reproduction of the black population at a time when they will double in numbers by the turn of the century. It is also most offensive that whites should be made to finance this reproduction.'

If the audience had been silent up till then, it was possible to hear a pin drop after Brandsma's interjection. John Peters shifted his weight.

'What exactly are you saying, Professor Brandsma? That I should withhold my treatment simply because my patients are black? Doesn't that conflict with the Hippocratic Oath?'

'I am not asking you to violate the Hippocratic Oath, Dr Peters,' Brandsma returned. 'What I am asking you to do is to consider for a moment just who is financing your generosity towards infertile black couples. It is whites. And it is those whites who will be driven into the sea as a result of your abuse of their generosity. It seems that it would be more just to use those resources to help white couples. After all, there are already more than enough blacks in South Africa.'

Peters's jaw dropped.

'Such racism has absolutely no place in medicine,' he blurted out. 'And if it has, we should close the hospital.'

Some members of the audience started clapping, but it soon petered out self-consciously.

Brandsma stood up and roared, 'Racism! Good God, man. I am only talking about common sense. When we whites are driven out, who will finance the treatment of your beloved blacks? Who will give them effective treatment? I refuse to be insulted any longer. You will have to preach your inverse racism without me!'

With that comment, Brandsma stormed out of the lecture theatre, banging the door behind him.

Peters stood there dumbfounded. Mercifully, the chairman got up and thanked Peters for his interesting presentation, reminding everyone of the guest lecture the following week.

The match was over.

CHAPTER 9

They were having lunch in the doctors' mess. The tension had given Neal a large appetite and he was wolfing down a plate of Boboti, while Jill was tucking into a tuna salad. The digestion of the heated exchange in the lecture hall was more difficult.

'The whole thing was staged, Neal,' Jill said between mouthfuls.

'How d'you mean?'

'Peters got a call this morning from Isaacs informing him that the hospital had cut the funds for his Infertility Clinic. I reckon Isaacs and Brandsma got together at the meeting to try to justify the cuts. But it sort of backfired.'

'Hmm. Either way, though, it looks like the Infertility Clinic will be hit. Brandsma is right in one regard. If the Afrikaner voters found out that their taxes were contributing to their problems, they would freak out. I guess Peters is lucky to have a black infertility clinic at all.'

Jill reluctantly agreed.

'You know, I can't understand one thing,' Neal continued. 'If Brandsma is so against blacks reproducing, how come he's an obstetrician?'

Jill laughed. 'I think he went into obstetrics to get them to stop reproducing. He's really aggressive with his birth control policy.'

Neal grinned. Then he remembered something.

'Changing the subject, what can you tell me about obesity and post-partum psychosis?'

'Talking shop. are we?' Jill teased.

'I plead guilty. But can you help?'

'I can tell you about obesity and post-partum hæmorrhage,' Jill said playfully.

'Sorry, it has to be post-partum psychosis. You know— madness, insanity, lunacy, away with the fairies, loopy, round the twist.'

'Ah yes. I think I've heard of that. But I think you are supposed to be the psychiatrist. Why?'

'It might not be anything significant. But I was looking up the cases of post-partum psychosis over the last year—so I could sound more informed when next you ask me to assess one of your patients. Most of them were obese primups. For the life of me, I can't see how obesity fits in. Any ideas?'

'Sorry, Neal. I don't have the foggiest how obesity can cause—what was it? Loopiness?'

Neal grinned at her. He was enjoying himself and didn't object.

'Nothing coming into that pretty head of yours?'

'No. However, I'm free for coffee at four.'

With that, Jill stood up and lifted her coat off the back of the seat.

'See you.'

'Sure.'

Neal would have to wait for an answer.

'Why the hell did you have to say there were already enough blacks around. Jesus, man! It's all very well to think it, but quite another thing to stand up and blurt it out before such an audience.'

Isaacs was angry, at himself more than anything. He had handled the meeting badly. He wiped the sweat off his brow with his handkerchief. There was enough heat around without Brandsma stoking the fire.

'Let me remind you which government gave you your job,' Brandsma thundered back.

'No. Let me remind you of something, Jannie-boy. I'm sticking my neck out for you, and to tell you the truth, it's getting a little stiff. Now you get a move on with things, all right? I don't have to remind you how bad it's going to look if someone finds out what you're doing, especially now you've blurted out your political views.'

Brandsma took hold of himself, saw the sense in what Isaacs was saying, and simmered down. He slumped into the chair and pulled at his goat's beard. His temper was his downfall.

'That Potter given you any trouble?' Isaacs changed the subject.

'Not yet, not yet. But I've got one of my boys on him.'

'Now, don't the cases sound a little strange?'

Jill, cupping her hands around a mug of coffee, looked quizzically back at Neal who was sitting next to her.

'Sorry, dear. I haven't a clue. After all, I'm only a lowly obstetric registrar. But if you'll pass me a copy of McDougal, we'll see what the expert says.'

Putting the mug of coffee on the floor, she balanced the large red volume on her knees and began thumbing through the index. She soon found the right page and read:

'"A number of features characterize post-partum psychosis. Firstly, the disorder is commonest amongst primups and has its onset mostly within the first two weeks of delivery, only very rarely within the first few days. Secondly, patients commonly suffer from delusions that the baby is deformed or dead. Thirdly, disorientation is common. Finally, patients frequently elaborate paranoid delusions that the staff are against them."'

Jill paused, pursing her lips.

'Uhuh. So what's bothering you is the fact that your cases are all obese and have visual hallucinations . . .'

'And they all start in the first forty-eight hours,' Neal completed her sentence.

'So what does Sherlock Holmes think?'

'Elementary . . .'

Neal's bleep sounded off. It was Chemical Pathology. He had forgotten about the investigations.

'Hallo, Mark. Have you got the results?'

Neal lifted his notebook from his coat pocket and jotted down the results, repeating them as he received them.

'Normal white count, normal electrolytes, normal liver enzymes. Hmm. Looks like I was wrong about it being the DT's, huh?'

He listened, and then laughed.

'Yes, I know. Psychiatrists have been known to make mistakes. Anyway, I'll catch you later. Thanks for the results.'

He replaced the receiver slowly, trying to digest the results.

'What made you think of DT's?'

'The visual hallucinations, I guess. But it's a dead end. Want some more coffee? Nothing like caffeine to stimulate the brain into action.'

Neal moved slowly towards the table by the window.

Suddenly he pulled himself up. He could have kicked himself.

'Nothing like caffeine to stimulate the brain,' he repeated. 'Christ! Drugs. I forgot to ask about drugs.'

After phoning the laboratory to order a drug screen on Selina Zondi's blood, he poured out the coffee. Leaving his mug on the table, he began pacing about. Experience had taught him that he did his best thinking on the move.

'Look, what about this? What if some Zulu pimp has his prostitutes hooked on hard drugs so that he has control of them? What if they are part of some prostitution racket in the Umfulosi Township? We all know Zulu men prefer ample buttocks, and this would explain why all the cases are obese, by our standards anyway. It would also explain why they are young, unmarried, end up pregnant, and have visual hallucinations as they withdraw from the drugs. What do you think?'

'Not bad,' Jill remarked.

'Sounds a little extraordinary, I know. But the drug screen will tell.'

'Not everything fits, Sherlock. What about the fact that they all pass through delivery suites 05 and 06?' Jill objected.

'Oh shit! And they all pass under the care of Brandsma. And end up at the Umzimkulu Rehabilitation Unit. I'd forgotten about that.'

He stopped pacing and stared blankly out the window.

'Some detective, huh? Anyway, what's your theory, Jill?'

'Sorry, Neal. I'm afraid I get most of my best ideas at night. Mostly around seven o'clock. After work.'

Neal grinned. 'Is that your place or mine?'

'Mine. Flat 48, Sea View, on the Marine Parade.'

Then she deposited her mug on the table and was gone.

Neal stared blankly after her. There was probably a simple explanation, but it didn't look like it was going to be the one he had just conjured. There was that awkward fact that the cases had passed through Brandsma's hands. Not to mention the fact he had been personally handling the suicide, and been so defensive about it. And then there was the disappearance of the notes on the other suicides. Something was fishy somewhere.

He focused his eyes on the scene outside the window. The sun was streaming in horizontally through the dirty glass pane, lighting up the dust particles floating in the room, and for a moment he forgot about the hospital and its problems.

For the last 36 hours he had been awake, and the effects of lack of sleep were beginning to tell. He rubbed his eyes till spots danced in front of him.

As his visual field assembled itself, he noticed the silhouette of a Zulu in a headdress across the courtyard. Neal closed his eyes again, wondering if he was over-fatigued and hallucinating.

When he opened his eyes again, the figure was gone.

CHAPTER 10

'That was a great dinner!'

Neal leaned back till his chair came to rest against the wall. He gazed through two wavering candles at the attractive woman sitting across the table. She was dressed in jeans with a silk blouse loosely following the contours of her body until it was drawn in at the waist with a scarf. But it was her face that was capturing his attention.

Jill looked up and blushed.

'OK. Now I'll tell you what I think,' Jill said awkwardly, sidetracking him.

'Think about what?' Neal asked innocently.

'The post-partum cases, silly.'

'Oh yes.' Neal sounded disappointed. 'Go ahead.'

Shifting his attention was difficult. But his disappointment was short-lived.

'I was never much good at this detective reasoning. But what about this for an inference? We know that Brandsma is pretty unhappy about blacks reproducing. We also know that a lot of black women in their reproductive years passing through his care end up either mad or dead. Now what better way to stop them from reproducing . . .?'

'Jesus!' Neal hissed through clenched teeth. 'That's some logic!'

'Pretty good, huh? At first I didn't take it too seriously. But then you said Brandsma was acting suspiciously, as if he was up to something.'

'Yes,' Neal said hesitantly. 'But being a racist doesn't amount to being a criminal, does it? I mean, it just sounds too fantastical. Too fictional. Too much like *Coma*. Next you'll be saying he is stealing their organs for white recipients! And there's another thing: how does he do it? Drive the women mad, I mean. You can't just wave a wand, you know . . .'

Jill looked glum, like a schoolgirl who had been caught cheating.

'I don't know, Neal. You don't know the man like I do.'

'Maybe not. But . . .'

'Anyway,' Jill interrupted. 'Like Sherlock Holmes said: when all possibilities have been eliminated, then what remains, however implausible, is the truth. Or something like that.'

It was Neal's turn to look glum. Hell! She had a point. And the theory did fit rather nicely. Too nicely. It was convenient that all the women were unmarried—no husbands to remove them from the asylum. And he too had come to know Brandsma while he had assisted at Cæsars for him. He knew the man was a fanatic.

Neal struggled to assemble the pieces.

'If Brandsma is doing this, how come he's only doing it with obese women? And how come it's only occurring in 05 and 06?'

'Easy. Brandsma is studying the complications of obesity in labour. And he's using those two delivery suites for the study.'

The theory seemed too good to be true.

'Look, in spite of what Sherlock said, if the remaining alternative is too implausible, there just has to be another explanation. I mean, no scientific theory about the origin of the universe seems right. But does that mean God made it?'

Jill laughed. 'You've a point there. I take it you are not the religious type?'

'I don't worship God, if that's what you mean.'

'What do you worship, then?' Jill asked innocently.

Neal sipped his wine. 'Do you want to know?' he continued mysteriously, quickly forgetting Brandsma and his patients.

'Now, I *am* intrigued.'

'Well, you see. I've only recently been converted. It was a kind of conversation experience, really. There I was, sitting quietly eating spaghetti, and I had a visitation.'

'An hallucination, you mean?' Jill was grinning now.

'Could have been, I suppose.' Neal put down his glass of wine. 'Except that it's persisted somewhat.'

'I'm still a bit confused about this religion,' Jill continued coyly. 'How do you go about this worshipping of yours?'

'Ah!' Neal grinned, and slowly pushed himself up from his chair, moved round to Jill's side. He put his finger under her chin, and gently raised her head to look at him. They were suddenly solemn again, staring at each other, scanning each other's face, looking for a statement, an affirmation.

Jill stood up and pushed her chair away. Then, as if drawn by a magnet, Neal bent forward, slowly at first, then accelerating as his lips neared hers. Her lips were warm and welcoming, saying yes to him, banishing any hesitation, thrilling him. He had forgotten about plots to keep blacks from reproducing. There were more important things.

Neal lost himself in the embrace. He could feel his skin tingle as her hands touched his shoulders, gently at first, and then with increasing passion. He drew himself away for a moment.

'I think I'll leave post-partum psychosis to somebody

else to study. The madness of common people is far more fascinating.'

'Don't think that that is lost on me, Mr Psychiatrist. I too have read my Freud. Are you telling me you're in love?'

Jill gently poked the tip of Neal's nose with her finger.

'Whatever gave you that idea?' Neal said, grinning. 'The madness of the common people is simply a passion for carrying beautiful women into their bedrooms. Like this.'

Neal lifted her into his arms, and carried her down the corridor towards her bedroom, where he lowered her gently on to the bed. The room was unlit, but the moon shone through the French windows and provided light enough, enough to illuminate Jill's dark eyes, her strong chin, the prominent line of her neck muscles, her breasts rising and falling rapidly.

Neal kissed her again, gently this time, moving to her ears, her neck, the small area of unopened blouse. Then he pulled back and looked at her.

'God, you're beautiful!' he whispered.

'Shhh.'

She pulled him down on top of her and they kissed again, her mouth open this time with her tongue playfully meeting his.

He disengaged himself, this time to unbutton her blouse. She pulled at his shirt. They were hungry. Their clothes were cast aside. They locked together, rolling, squeezing, exploring.

Then he was inside her.

At first he couldn't move. It was too pleasurable, and the moment had to be savoured, made to last. He wanted time to stop.

Then they began to move together, slowly, but with controlled passion. Neal's muscles taut, his movements measured, Jill holding on fiercely, crying out with each thrust, digging her fingers into his muscular back.

'Oh god!'

Neal's muscles seized in a convulsion of pleasure. Jill

stretched out, as if to reach up and grasp for something. Then she grabbed Neal in a stranglehold, crying out.

When it was over, they stayed locked together.

Jill whispered: 'Now I understand.'

'Understand?'

'About your religion.'

Nongoma slipped on the blue overalls he had taken from the changing-rooms. A brief check confirmed the plastic bottles and syringes in the large pockets. After glancing with approval at his disguise in the mirror, he moved off in search of a trolley.

One was lying in the middle of the corridor in Casualty, abandoned no doubt by a porter keen to catch the last township bus home. Nongoma soon had the trolley running towards the lifts. It would not take him long to get to Level 15.

He watched the light illuminate the numbers in turn while he thought of what he had to do. Performing the exchange in hospital was a lot more dangerous, but the white man had to be stopped. Then the light reached No. 15 and he got out.

The corridor was deserted. No one to ask him what he was doing there. There were moaning and grunting noises coming from the delivery suites. Women in labour. Yet it sounded like hell. It sounded like a torture chamber.

'That is exactly what it is,' Nongoma said under his breath, reminding himself of his purpose. 'A chamber to poison the mind.'

He pushed forward, sensing traces of Selina's anguish. When he felt it at its strongest, he found himself outside 05.

'Can I help?'

There was a plump white man in a suit standing in the middle of the empty theatre. It was Isaacs.

'I was bleeped to pick up a patient in 05, Doctor,' Nongoma faltered. 'Someone else got here before me?'

'There's been no woman in labour here for the last four hours. Must be a mistake.'

Isaacs turned away. Then he suddenly froze.

'What's your name, boy?' he asked as he swung around.

Isaacs was not ready for the reply. Nongoma ran forward dragging the trolley with him. When he had taken three strides within the theatre, he flung all his weight behind the trolley, sending it spinning towards the white man.

The heavy missile caught Isaacs in the solar plexus as it spun, knocking him off his feet and on to the tiled floor.

Nongoma did not wait to see the result. He was content to hear the loud crack as a head made contact with tiles.

His work would have to wait.

It was a while before Isaacs picked himself slowly and painfully up off the cold surgical floor.

'That just about does it,' he murmured to himself. 'I've had enough.'

He struggled to the door and leaned against the frame, catching his panting breath.

'And a bloody kaffir to boot,' he spat. 'Brandsma isn't going to be pleased. His work being jeopardized is one thing. But the whole thing being ruined by a black man!'

He shook his head and staggered out of 05.

It was time to reconsider.

CHAPTER 11

When Neal awoke he was alone. There was sudden panic. Where was Jill? Had she left him? Had last night really happened?

Everything was quiet, like a silent movie. It felt as if he were a spectator, passive, impotent to change the inevitability of events.

Somehow he knew he would find Jill on the veranda. He moved slowly out into the moonlight, and saw them at the far end. They seemed locked in a close embrace. No, tussle. Jill was fighting someone off, someone big, solid, with coarse features shining with sweat. It was Brandsma. And he was trying to push her over the balcony.

'It's Brandsma after all,' Neal heard himself think.

He tried to launch himself to her rescue. But he stood transfixed, immobilized. His mouth opened, but there was no sound. All he could do was watch as they got closer and closer to the edge, watch as Jill was forced over, watch as her body plunged earthwards.

Even that did not galvanize him. It was only when he heard the ambulance's siren that he could move.

He shot forward and found himself bolt upright in Jill's bedroom, terror in his heartbeat, with the sheet sticking to his drenched body.

If it had not been for the continued bleeping, he would have orientated himself sooner. He did not know what it was until he recognized the sound of his bleep, and for once in his life he welcomed the disturbance. He leaned over the bed and groped in his jacket pocket to switch it off.

Jill was stirring beside him, and he delicately kissed her on the forehead. She opened her eyes, smiled, and stretched her arms around his neck in a warm embrace.

'Did I hear a bleep, or was I dreaming?'

'It was a dream, thank God. Where is the phone?'

Jill frowned at his comment, but indicated the drawer in her bedside table before curling up to snatch another five minutes' sleep.

'I wonder who can be bleeping me at seven in the morning?' he thought aloud.

'Dr Potter on 837.' He paused. 'Thanks.' If he was not awake earlier, he was certainly awake now. It was McKenzie, and Neal remembered the drug screen.

'Neal, old boy, sorry to disturb you at this ungodly hour, but I am going off duty and thought you might be interested.' The line was crackling, but Neal's senses were acute.

'No problem. What have you got?'

'Spectacular news. I screened her serum, and guess what I found? No, don't worry, I won't wait for you to get it.

Lysergic Acid Diethylamide. Commonly known as LSD.
Well, at least that's what I think it is. And a hallucinogenic
dose of it at that . . . You still there?'

'Yes, I'm still here. Stunned, but here. You said "I think".
Is there any doubt?'

'LSD is the nearest match the spectrometer could make,
so I'm not a hundred per cent sure. It would help if you could
get hold of a sample of LSD from the Psychopharmacology
Department so that I can calibrate my machine properly.
It may be malfunctioning.'

'Sure . . .'

'Thanks. I'll catch you later. I must get some sleep now.
I just thought you would be interested to know straight
away. Was I right, or was I right?'

'Right, as usual. Thanks a million. I'll speak to you later.'

Neal replaced the receiver thoughtfully. It was getting
more and more confusing by the day. He got out of bed and
made for the shower. As soon as he climbed under the water,
he was joined by Jill. He let his eyes explore her body,
enjoying their closeness.

'Who bleeped you?' Jill asked after a while, pushing him
away playfully.

'It was Mark. He ran a drug screen on the patient with
post-partum psychosis, and found LSD floating around in
her veins. Pretty interesting, huh?'

'Can LSD trigger a psychotic illness?' Jill asked, suddenly
fascinated too.

'I think a bad trip could certainly mimic a psychotic
illness. But I reckon it could only trigger a schizophrenic
illness in someone with a family history of schizophrenia.'

'Remind me not to take it,' Jill whispered.

'Huh?'

Jill had suddenly become quiet.

'I have an aunt who has paranoid schizophrenia. She was
admitted to Constantia lunatic asylum a while back, and
has never come out.'

'I'm sorry,' Neal said, not knowing exactly what he was
apologizing for.

'Don't be sorry,' Jill perked up, pushing the image of her aunt to the back of her mind. 'Not taking LSD is no great hardship.'

Neal calculated the risk of Jill becoming ill. Although he knew Jill was twice as likely as normal to become schizophrenic, thankfully that meant only a two per cent chance. Too small a risk to worry about. He dismissed the spectre from his mind.

Instead he began to wonder whether the other post-partum cases were caused by LSD. Like effects should have like causes.

Then he remembered the two-month rule. The hospital had adopted the policy of keeping any blood left over from laboratory investigations for two months after each patient was discharged. Just in case some investigation had been neglected. Or someone wanted to do some research.

He flung himself out of the shower, dragged on his clothes, and after promising to meet Jill later in the day, headed for the door.

There was work to do.

CHAPTER 12

The laboratory technician was being infuriatingly slow. Or, things being relative, Neal Potter was becoming increasingly impatient.

He had flown down the Marine Parade in his old Fiat 124, and a few narrow misses had only raised to saturation level the adrenalin flowing through his arteries. What he didn't need now was a phlegmatic, half-asleep bureaucrat.

'What do you mean, I have to have an A3 clearance?' Neal thundered, banging the desk with his fist.

'*Kyk hier, ou. Dis nie my probleem nie.*'

The large and slow Afrikaner was standing firm.

Neal hated the Afrikaans language. It was so guttural and coarse, and when it was used to indicate that English was beneath the speaker's dignity, it made him even more mad.

'Listen here. I don't give a damn about your A3 clearances. The hospital administrator, Dr Isaacs, asked me to run a bilirubin on Rachel Dlamini. Now do you want to lose your job, or are you going to get me the sample of blood?'

The name of the hospital administrator was like a bell to one of Pavlov's dogs. The thickset laboratory technician bit his lip, glared suspiciously at Neal, and then finally swung the clearance book around to face him.

'*Teken hier.*' He stabbed his finger at the bottom of the page, and moved sullenly off towards the back of the laboratory.

Neal paced up and down after signing his name in the book. If Dlamini's blood contained LSD, what did it all mean? He watched the second hand trudge slowly round the laboratory clock while he felt his blood pressure rise. Eventually he could stand it no longer.

Lifting the hinged counter, Neal headed towards the refrigerated storeroom at the back of the laboratory, almost breaking into a run. When he reached the door, the laboratory technician all but knocked him over as he pushed his way out.

'Now just wait a minute. You have no right . . .' the large man spluttered.

'I told you Dr Isaacs was in a hurry. I . . . we haven't any time to waste. Now where is the sample?'

'Listen, Doctor,' the technician sounded apologetic. 'It just isn't there. Are you sure her discharge date was—'

'Shit!' Neal swore. The day was not proceeding as well as it had started. He tore the laboratory book out of the bewildered technician's hands and searched for the name 'Rachel Dlamini'. It was in the middle of the second page. 'Discharge date: December 27. Folder number: F2569435. Laboratory rack: E79a.'

'Let's go,' he ordered, pushing the bigger man back into the fridge. Although the man was clearly annoyed, Neal knew that the threat of authority was keeping him in check.

It was chilly in there, and Neal could feel the ripple of gooseflesh move up his back. He shuddered, and followed the technician's shiny bald patch into the semi-dark, gazing at row upon row of red glowing tubes.

The man turned down one of the side corridors and stopped by the shelf marked 'E79'. He took out the first rack, handing it to Neal to see for himself. Neal painstakingly went through each tube, checking the name and number with the book, double checking.

There was no blood sample with Dlamini's folder number.

'Has anyone else requisitioned the samples?' Neal demanded angrily.

The surly laboratory technician put the rack back on the shelf without a word, turned, and led the way out of the cold interior.

'See for yourself.' He shoved the book into Neal's abdomen. If Neal had not been so concerned about the possibility of a further cover-up, he would have noticed the technician's insulting manner.

He followed his thumb down two months of signatures. There was no request for Rachel Dlamini's blood. Neal checked again. And again. There was nothing. He turned his stare to the technician, trying to intimidate him.

'Who else has access?'

'The lab shifts have access, and so does the Professor of Chemical Pathology. The administrator has a master key too.'

'Hmm.'

The hospital administrator was cropping up again. And in all the wrong places.

He turned slowly round, leaving the laboratory without thanking the perplexed technician. He was too lost in thought to notice the technician reach furtively for the phone.

'Boss, it's me. From the lab.'

Pause.

'Ja, I know you said I shouldn't phone you during the day.'

Another pause.

'I'm sorry, OK? But I thought you said if there was anything urgent . . .'

The laboratory technician scratched his bald patch while he listened to the angry voice on the line.

'There was a Dr Potter here.' He read the name off the request book. 'He was after a sample of Rachel Dlamini's blood. I thought you ought to know.'

Pause.

'Did I hear you right? Isn't that a bit radical? I mean, all he wants to do is some blood tests.'

It wasn't that the technician didn't like the idea. He hadn't enjoyed being pushed around by the snotty-nosed doctor. It was just that he couldn't understand it.

'OK, boss. I'll let you do the thinking. How do you want it done?'

The laboratory technician grinned as he listened to the plan. He was going to enjoy it.

When Neal arrived at the psychiatric wards there were casually dressed nurses and patients milling in the corridor. He was relieved that he no longer had to play the game 'Guess the Patient'.

The informality of the ward was not something for which he had been prepared, and he remembered with embarrassment the day he had mistaken a sane-looking patient for a nurse and asked for a report. The patient had handled it well, and had given a plausible account of how everyone was coming along, including himself. The prejudice that insanity could be read from the face had been quick to disappear.

He went straight into the doctor's office to retrieve Selina Zondi's notes from the filing cabinet. Some preparation had to be done for the ward round.

It was soon eight o'clock, and the ward staff filed into the seminar room, seating themselves in a circle in the middle

of the room. Psychiatric ward rounds were different from
standard medical rounds. Nobody went round to see the
patients, not physically anyway. It was a ward round in the
head, a mental round, as Neal used to pun.

Professor Dirk Evans, a short stocky man who resembled
a friendly bear, with a walrus moustache, humorous brown
eyes, and rosy cheeks that made him the brunt of jokes about
alcoholism, opened the meeting and asked the registrars to
present the new cases. Neal's was last.

When Neal came to present, the energies of the staff were
flagging. Neal decided to keep it brief and stick to the facts.
Anyway, the Professor did not like speculation. Some of
Neal's enthusiasm for the unusual case conveyed itself to
the ward round, reviving fading powers of concentration.

'Special Investigations have demonstrated a level of .5
micrograms of lysergic acid diethylamide in her blood. A
diagnosis of drug-induced hallucinosis, suggested by the
clinical picture, is thus confirmed,' Neal ended.

'Very interesting case, Neal. May I compliment you on
sticking to your clinical intuitions about the case and running a drug screen.'

Evans did not let him bathe in glory for long.

'Nevertheless, do not ignore the possibility that the abuse
of the drug has caused a psychotic illness. My impression
is that the drug has precipitated schizophrenia rather than
simply mimicking it,' Professor Evans cautioned. 'Can I
have the nurse's report?'

A staff nurse then gave an account of the patient's stormy
and frenzied course over the last 36 hours.

'There you are. Her current picture is overwhelmingly
against the diagnosis you are offering. Do you know the
half-life of LSD?'

'I've not tried it, Prof.' Neal made light of his oversight.
It was a trick that he had cultivated over the years, and it
had stood him in good stead.

The round collapsed in laughter, and the ruddy face of
the professor of psychiatry broke into a huge grin. He knew
he had lost the first round.

'About time you got some experience of what it is like to hallucinate. The half-life is eight hours. Which means it ought to have been completely excreted. Nevertheless, she continues to hallucinate and remains as deluded as ever. It is most unlikely that she is still having a bad trip.'

Neal, in spite of his witty counter, felt deflated. Evans was probably right.

'Nevertheless, you have no doubt isolated an important etiological factor. Remember rule number two is: Run a drug screen when a patient sees pink elephants.'

The staff laughed. One of the registrars asked: 'Prof, what is rule number one?'

'Take regular coffee breaks. And it's about time we put it into effect.'

Neal sat thinking while the rest of the staff filed out. There was something wrong with Evans's reasoning but he could not put his finger on it.

'At least we can test his theory,' he said aloud.

He enlisted the help of one of the male nurses and the two of them entered the acute corridor.

The title 'Acute Corridor' had originally evoked images of Bedlam in Neal's mind: padded cells, screaming patients struggling in strait-jackets, nurses in white coats with sets of keys chained to their waists, prison-like regimen, and frequent physical confrontations between staff and patients.

But the major tranquillizers like chlorpromazine had changed all that. In the last 30 years a chemical strait-jacket had made the old madhouses obsolete. The modern acute corridor was like any other ward. The only difference was that there was only one way out, a path guarded night and day by a nurse on duty.

Selina Zondi was completely flattened by the heavy doses of drugs. She hardly responded when Neal drove the needle into her vein, letting the vacuum in the tube suck out the blood. There was only a moan and a weak withdrawal reflex.

While Neal was labelling the sample, his pager emitted

the rapid pulse for an emergency. He had forgotten he was covering for the wards during the day. He quickly found a phone.

'Dr Potter here.'

'Hallo. Thanks for the prompt reply. This is Staff Nurse Smith from Surgical 3. We have a frenzied patient on the run. Looks psychotic. He's landed up in the boiler room. Can you come and help?'

'Sure,' Neal replied. 'Can you and a colleague—preferably a male nurse—meet me there? I'll bring some sedation.'

The ward pharmacy was on the way out. In a few minutes he had stuffed a few ampoules of Paraldehyde into his pocket, together with a syringe and a couple of needles. He was now ready.

The boiler room was in the basement of the hospital, tucked away beneath the Chemical Pathology Laboratory. Neal had to consult one of the many hospital maps posted on every floor to locate it. As soon as he knew where to go, he thundered down the stairs, taking two at a time. The lifts would have been too busy.

After nearly knocking a patient off his trolley, Neal made it to the basement. He had expected to find male nurse Smith waiting for him, but there was no one. Just an empty corridor ending at a large metal door signposted 'Boiler Room'.

Neal paused and shook his head. 'They are probably trying to contain him inside,' he panted aloud, grateful for the moment to catch his breath.

He walked up to the metal door breathing deeply to expel the accumulated carbon dioxide. The boiler room was not locked, and as Neal heaved the door open, he could feel the blast of hot air.

He peered through the steamy room, just discerning the large copper sphere in front of him and the large pipes extending like tentacles from the metallic body to the wards above. Built into the far wall was the control panel consisting of numerous levers and dials.

There was no sign of the nurses.

'Or the patient,' Neal thought aloud. 'Maybe he has fled elsewhere.'

Neal waited in the sea of steam, sweeping the room slowly, looking for any sign of movement, any sign of life. His ears strained, but all he could hear was the hissing of the pressure valve.

Had he got the message right? Was it the boiler room? He decided he would await a further bleep. There was no point in searching the whole hospital.

It was just at that moment that he turned around and straight into the glancing blow of something very, very hard.

If Neal had not turned at that moment, he would undoubtedly have been unconscious. Maybe even dead. A lead pipe can do awful things to the human skull, especially if it is swung through a large enough arc. In fact, if the right suture line is selected, the outcome is almost certainly fatal. As it happened, Neal was struck a glancing blow to the back of his head and thrown backwards.

Neal crashed back on to one of the radiating pipes, bouncing off again like India rubber on to the floor. For an instant he was blinded from the jar to his visual cortex, but mercifully not disorientated. He had come prepared to tackle a disturbed patient, and he had not been disappointed. Some mental preparation had been done, and instinctively he rolled over. There was no point presenting a stationary target.

It was just in time. The lead pipe crashed into the floor, shattering a tile into pieces that flew everywhere, stinging the side of Neal's face. As he rolled over, he caught sight of the pyjama-clad legs standing astride in a pair of gold-buckled brown boots.

A delayed wave of pain surged over Neal's head, catching him off guard. He gasped. He wanted to yell, to close his eyes. There wasn't time. He was fortunate that his body was doing the thinking. Somehow it assessed the situation, saw the legs advance, and scrambled under the copper pipe out of sight.

Once on the other side, he slithered on the slippery floor, heart in his mouth, and ran towards the boiler, his body doubled over, sticking close to the pipe for cover. If he could reach the boiler, he knew he had a chance.

He dared not look round. Any delay could be fatal. And there was his balance to retain. He could not afford to make mistakes.

His brain started functioning again. The odd-numbered wards contained black patients. So his attacker was black. Strong. And judging from the footsteps hammering after him, a big fellow. Armed with some truncheon or other. Probably paranoid. And very dangerous.

Neal made a mental note to retire from psychiatry if he got out of there alive. Then he was at the ladder.

At the back of the boiler was an aluminium ladder curving up the side of the great copper sphere. It was narrow and difficult to climb even if one was not in a hurry, and Neal had no intention of loitering.

His sweaty palms hissed as he began scrambling up. At first he hardly noticed, but soon the heat was unbearable. Then the pain made up his mind. Enough was enough. He had to waste agonizing moments while he retreated his hands into the shells of his coat sleeves. All the time he kept his eye on the pressure valve. He was half way there.

Then a large hand closed around his foot. He kicked frantically in a futile attempt to shake himself free. He was held fast. He suppressed the urge to scream out for help, to try to reason with his assailant. Help was not at hand, and there was no point trying to reason with paranoia.

He kicked again. Still the hand held on. It was time to try something else. Suspending himself from his hands, he used his free foot to try to lever off his captive shoe. Sweating heavily now, sucking in air in sharp gasps, he battled to get it off, his mind numbed with fear.

Then it was off. He was free. Another six rungs and he was above the pressure valve. This was the moment. He looked down and waited.

The patient moved upwards, and for a second time Neal

felt the fierce grip around his ankle. For a moment the patient lifted up his head and glared at Neal. Over his head was a stocking which flattened his features into an ugly mask.

Neal drove his free foot down on the pressure valve, releasing the steam with a piercing hiss. It all but drowned the scream from his assailant. Neal felt the grip loosen, saw the man's squashed face contort with pain, and watched him disappear beneath a jet of steam.

Neal kept his foot jammed on the valve as if to guarantee that the man remained permanently out of sight. After a while, he released the pressure and peered tentatively over the bulge of the boiler at the floor. Ther was no sign of his assailant.

'Oh shit!'

He waited and watched, but no movement betrayed the man's presence. He didn't really want to move. There was something secure about having such a vantage-point. It gave him time to think.

Patient in a stocking? Very odd. And the nurses? Unconscious? Or dead?

Neal shook his head. He could not stay up there all day. Gingerly at first, then more hurriedly, he retreated down the ladder. Still nothing. He paused briefly. Was he in the clear?

Then he was unable to prevent himself from doing a disappearing act. He vaulted over the waist-high pipe and ran for the door. He was soon in the corridor, up the stairs, and among ordinary people.

'Jesus!' He exhaled with inexpressible relief. 'And they said psychiatry was tame!'

Once he had recovered, he had to think about some more awkward facts.

'*Lewe Hemel!* What happened to you?'

Brandsma strode up to the desk and leaned over to take a closer look, turning his head on the side and leering.

'Had a fight with your wife again, man?' he teased.

Isaacs shuffled uneasily in his chair. There was at least one consolation in boasting two black eyes. He couldn't be blamed for not stopping such a vicious psychopath.

'We're up against a vicious psychopath,' he began explaining.

'It's taken you all this time to get to know what your wife is like, then?' Brandsma continued, guffawing at his already stale jibe.

Isaacs shot up in his chair to impose a tone of seriousness on the conversation, but immediately regretted it, his brow furrowing suddenly, his hand straying up to his head. He sat down again.

'Jan,' Isaacs began. 'I want out. Let's wrap this thing up now, shall we?'

Brandsma sat down, deciding it was not the time to mention Isaacs divorcing his wife.

'What happened, then?'

Isaacs told the story about his encounter with the porter, and the trolley. And the floor. He elaborated somewhat, the porter quickly becoming armed, and attacking him from behind.

Brandsma's expression became serious. He tugged at his beard.

'I reckon there's two of them. At least. It doesn't look good.'

'How's that?'

'You don't think the kaffir could have figured it out all on his own, do you?'

Isaacs shook his head, immediately regretting it. He wasn't really listening. He knew he was in too deep to get out.

'A disturbed patient?' The large black sister looked up from the drugs trolley and shook her head.

'This is Surgical 3, isn't it?'

'Yessir, that's the one.'

'Well, half an hour ago I had a call from a staff nurse Smith about a disturbed patient.'

'Nosir, like I told you. You got the wrong ward. There's no disturbed patient here. And no staff nurse Smith.'

Neal combed his fingers through his hair.

'Maybe he is a locum?'

'Nosir. I'm in charge here, and I know's who's on, permanent staff or no. Like I told you, we don't have no staff nurse Smith. And no disturbed patients.'

The sister was getting irritated, so Neal did not press her. He had heard enough.

He needed to take sinister plots more seriously.

CHAPTER 13

'Cedric Zondi? Please come in.'

Neal got up from behind his desk, still buried under eighteen hospital folders, and came round to shake the elderly man's hand.

'How do you do?'

'*Nkosi.*' The old man bowed.

Neal showed him into the extra chair he had brought into his office for the interview.

'I wanted to speak to you about Selina. She is your daughter?' Neal began.

'Granddaughter, Doctor.' Cedric Zondi held his hat in his hand and looked straight at Neal.

'Your granddaughter is quite ill at the moment with a disease of the brain, but our medicines are controlling it. So rest assured on that count. But she will have to stay in hospital for a few weeks till she recovers, and then she should be able to return home. There is a fair chance that she will be able to lead a more or less normal life.'

The old man shook his head. 'I beg to question your word, Doctor. But illness of the brain? I think not.'

Neal wondered whether he should try to bridge the cultural divide, and for a moment he decided against it. His experience of trying to do it had not been very encouraging. But then he wondered whether the old man would be able to throw any light on the case. So he asked the grandfather to explain.

'It is the tokolosh, Doctor. It has penetrated the midst of our family, I fear, through my turning my back on the witch doctor. It first began when we sent Gordon, my great-grandson, to the white clinic for his vaccinations. The witch doctor had been furious that we had turned our backs on him and warned that the tokolosh would punish us. A week later Gordon was struck down with the Battle Cry Cough.'

Tears collected in the old man's eyes and Neal let him recover.

'But then Selina became ill with cramping pains, and we knew that the work of the tokolosh was not over. I decided that the time had come for reconciliation, so I sent Selina back to the witch doctor.'

Cedric paused, and took a deep breath.

'Things went well at first. Selina seemed to be getting better. But then the cramps started to build, and I knew the medicine man had abandoned us, that he was encouraging the tokolosh to possess Selina, and that our only hope was to come to you for help.'

Neal hesitated, wondering whether he should adopt the paternalistic stance and explain that there was no such thing as the tokolosh. But he decided to translate 'tokolosh' as 'disease process' and probe further.

'That may be true, Mr Zondi. But the medicine we are giving her will drive the tokolosh out.'

Cedric Zondi nodded his head. He had heard of the mighty medicine of the white man. Even the witch doctor had incorporated some of the white man's medicine into his arsenal of eagles' eyes and snakes' heads. He hoped that the white doctor was not speaking with the hyena's tongue. He had lost enough grandchildren already.

'May I ask a question about the personal life of your granddaughter?' Neal probed gently.

Cedric looked up for a moment, puzzled. Then he nodded.

'Did Selina have any men friends?' Neal wanted to test the theory that Selina was part of a prostitution racket.

Cedric frowned, puzzled at the question.

'She did have one young man visit her. Ai, ai, ai. A good boy, no *tsotsi*. He was from a good family too—they were collecting a *lobola* of ten cows for Selina. She was to be married to him next year.' He shook his head at what was lost.

Neal could tell from the old man's eyes that he was telling the truth. It was no profile of a prostitute.

'May I ask a question?' It was Cedric Zondi's turn.

'Go ahead.'

'Well, you see, it is rather difficult.' The old man looked away.

'Mr Zondi, I am here to help.'

'It is just that the witch doctor has warned me that the white man's medicine is poison. He says it calls in the tokolosh. He says Selina is not the first . . .'

Neal sat up in his chair.

'*Nkosi*,' Zondi apologized, 'I see you are offended. I feared you would see it this way. It is not that I mean to accuse. It is just that I don't know whom to trust.'

Neal wasn't listening. White man's medicine is poison. He was beginning to believe it.

'I'm afraid it is true.'

'Hau! Nongoma is right.'

'No. He is right to say that there are other women who have the same disease. But it has not been caused by our medicine,' Neal said uncomfortably.

Cedric was not reassured. He could see that the white man spoke the language of the hyena. Heaven help his Selina. He hung his head.

Neal sensed the gap opening up between them, not knowing quite what to do about it. He changed the subject.

'Now, do you think that your household will be able to cope with your new great-grandson?'

The old man nodded.

'I think it best if you take him with you—I am sure he is not the work of the tokolosh, so look after him well. Selina is in no fit state to care for him. There is some special milk-powder the nurses will give you to help with the feeding. Is there anything else you might need?'

Cedric Zondi shook his head and, taking the cue, rose from his chair.

Neal showed him to the door, reassuring him again that his medicine was no poison. But as he watched him go, his shoulders sagged with the thought that white medicine might well be driving Selina mad.

Nongoma was waiting for Cedric at the bus station.

They walked in silence for most of the way back to Zondi's home. It was not necessary for Nongoma to question the old man. The man's demeanour said it all.

Finally Zondi countered his reluctance to communicate.

'You were right.'

'Hmm.'

'Selina was not the first. The white medicine man admitted as much. But he said it was not his medicine . . .'

'The hyena's tongue talking.'

'Yes. It seemed that way to me. But I am sure it was not him.'

Nongoma laughed coldly.

'You talk to yourself with the hyena's tongue, Zondi. You try to make yourself more comfortable.'

Zondi sighed. It felt like his arms were too stiff to swing, his legs too heavy to lift, his heart too sore to beat. He did not care any more about the war between the two medicines. All he wanted was Selina's health.

'You must help, Zondi. You must help me save our people. Save Selina.' Nongoma had been reading his mind.

Zondi nodded slowly.

'How can I help?'

*

Neal found McKenzie in the Chemical Pathology Laboratory playing with molecules.

'How's it going?'

McKenzie looked up briefly before pipetting some clear fluid into a test-tube.

'Oh, OK, I suppose. I won't bore you with the details. How's your LSD lady?'

'Still freaked out, I'm sorry to say.'

'That's odd for a bad trip. Should be all over in twenty-four hours.' McKenzie looked thoughtful.

'Ja, I know. Prof Evans reckons she has schizophrenia.'

It was then that he knew what had been bothering him.

'Hold on,' Neal thought aloud. 'If Selina is having a schizophrenic illness, wouldn't you expect it to resemble schizophrenia?' It was a rhetorical question. 'So how come her illness continues to look like a bad trip? After all, it is one of Prof's rules that visual hallucinations undermine the diagnosis of schizophrenia. And Selina continues to have visual hallucinations. So it can't be schizophrenia . . .'

Neal paused, trying to think. If it wasn't a bad trip, and it wasn't schizophrenia, what in heaven's name was it?

McKenzie had a suggestion.

'Perhaps there are impurities in the LSD she took, making it difficult to dislodge from her brain, resulting in a permanent psychotic state.'

'That's a brilliant suggestion.'

'As I said over the phone, the mass spectrometer wasn't sure it was LSD. So perhaps it is some unusual isomer of LSD. Which reminds me, don't forget that sample you promised me.'

'I won't. Talking of samples . . .'

He produced the tube containing Selina's blood.

'When you have a moment can you see whether Selina still has LSD in her blood?'

'Sure thing.'

'If it will make it any easier, hold off for a moment. I am going to try to get another sample.'

'Another case come in?' McKenzie asked incredulously.

'No. I am off to see how the women have fared in the Umzimkulu Rehabilitation Unit.'

CHAPTER 14

The route to the Umzimkulu Rehabilitation Unit was along a dirt road that wound its way up the coast. Tall cliffs rose up from sandy beaches where the Indian Ocean pounded noisily. Sugar cane grew in abundance on either side of the road, blowing in the wind. As Neal drove along, dust billowed out from behind his Fiat 124, obscuring his vision to the rear.

'Lucky I'm not stuck behind some farm truck ferrying sugar cane to the mills,' Neal murmured.

He wanted to get to the Unit early so he wouldn't have to make his way back in the dark. It was bad enough negotiating the single track in the day.

He slowed to let a picanin cross the road with his cattle, easing slowly into the mass of suspicious animals. The young Zulu boy gave him a winning smile, but quickly returned his attention to his noisy and disobedient herd, cracking his whip over the backs of the snorting beasts, who surged round both sides of the car, giving Neal the impression that he was floating on a sea of cattle. And then the waves parted and he was able to ease his car forward once more.

Umzimkulu Rehabilitation Unit was set on a hill over-looking the sea. It had been a mission hospital at one time, the tell-tale chapel still dominating the site. The rest of the Unit consisted of four self-contained buildings situated in a square around the chapel. They were built in the Cape Dutch tradition with prominent gables, high ceilings, tall ceiling-to-floor windows, and wide barnlike doors.

It had a peaceful feel about it. In fact, it looked almost deserted as Neal drove through the open gates. Its dilapidated state lent weight to its ghostlike status. There were

huge chunks of flaking paint scabbing the surface of buildings, exposing bare brick beneath. Wooden shutters hung
loosely from their hinges, and ivy was invading the building
like a cancer.

He pulled the car to a skidding stop on the gravel road
in front of the nearest hospital block. Slipping his dark
glasses beneath the sun guard, he left his now dusty Fiat
and made his way up the steps.

Even the entrance to the building looked neglected. The
sun had penetrated the thin protective skin of the large
oaken doors, drying and splitting the wood. At the entrance
was a tarnished brass lever, which Neal assumed was the
bell. He rang it, carefully listening for any sign of life inside
the building. There was nothing.

He rang again. Still no sound could be heard from the
interior. He looked around the site for further evidence
of occupation. It looked derelict and unused, and Neal
wondered if there had been some mistake. He tried the door,
and it gave way noisily, the creaks echoing in the tiled
hallway.

The door opened on an entrance hall dominated by the
bust of some figure Neal did not recognize and did not
care to examine. There were three corridors leading off at
right-angles, and as there was nothing to choose between
them, Neal took the one on the left.

It was dark, punctuated by regular pillars on either side.
He moved slowly, his senses strained for any sound. There
was none.

He spotted her a split second before she moved, and he
sprang back like an uncoiled spring, stifling a cry in his
throat. She emerged from behind one of the pillars and
grabbed Neal's arm, drawing him towards her with a frenzied force. The grip on his arm was fierce, for the woman
was large and was animated by some unknown terror. He
instinctively wanted to shake her off and to run as fast as
he could out of the building. But his faculties were returning
rapidly, and he dismissed imagined horrors to the recesses
of his mind, holding his nerve.

He could see now that she was a patient and probably harmless. She was dressed in a loosely fitting gown which was tied in surgeon-style at the back. But it was her eyes rather than her dress that confirmed to Neal that she was a patient. She had a crazed stare, looking through Neal rather than at him.

'Please, baas, take me from this place,' the woman pleaded.

'Why?' Neal's voice sounded shaky and hoarse.

'They have raped me, Doctor. They string me up, spread my legs, then they rape me. Now I am pregnant. Look.'

The woman pulled her gown to expose one of her large breasts, and gave it a squeeze, and then another squeeze in a milking movement. Yellow-white liquid soon began to ooze from her nipple, running down her black breast and staining the gown.

'Look! You see! I am with child!' the black woman screamed. 'They have brought the tokolosh to rape me!'

The obese woman began tugging Neal's arm violently, chanting in Zulu, and shaking her head rhythmically from side to side. Neal had to hold on to the pillar to prevent himself being pulled over.

'Rachel! Come here at once!' The command was barked from Neal's shoulder, making him jump for the second time.

A bull-necked man in a white coat pushed himself past Neal, not caring to apologize, and forcibly pulled the woman away, casting an angry look in Neal's direction before he led her protesting loudly down the corridor.

Neal guessed that this was the nursing officer. His manner did not seem well suited to caring for mentally disturbed patients, but the authority he exhibited indicated that this was his job. He looked as though he belonged in some nineteenth-century asylum where a less sympathetic view of patients was taken.

Neal watched the pair disappear down the corridor, wondering what to do. There was one thing that was clear. His presence there wasn't appreciated.

Then the officer returned. He was big and solidly built.

His face was scarred from acne, and his hair was short-cropped, giving him the appearance of a convict. The scar on his cheek and the tattoo on his forearm completed the picture.

'*Kan ek jou help?*' The offer of help was in the words only. The tone was threatening.

'Er, well, I'm Dr Potter, a psychiatrist,' Neal said haltingly, extending his hand.

It hung suspended and unwelcomed for a few moments before Neal returned it to his side. Undeterred, he continued:

'Some of my patients were discharged here, and I have come to see how they have been progressing.'

'Davies.' The nurse introduced himself, still not extending his hand. 'Nursing officer.'

There was a pause as Davies stared hard at Neal as if to extract his real intentions, as if to intimidate him. Neal shifted his position, waiting.

'Have you made an appointment?'

'No,' Neal answered apologetically. 'I'm afraid I couldn't find your phone number in the directory. The government has recently appointed a commission to assess the adequacy of our rehabilitation facilities, and I'm part of the team checking on Natal's long-term psychiatric services.'

Neal paused before continuing the deception.

'I'm doing this by following up the patients admitted to Wellington. Some I believe have been rehabilitated here.'

'What patients?'

'Rachel Dlamini, Elsie Makeezwa, and Miriam Umbuti.'

'You have seen Rachel. Let me take you to Miriam. Elsie is sleeping right now, and you will not be able to see her.' The tone conveyed finality.

With that, he turned around and led the way back down the corridor. Neal almost had to run to keep up.

'Rachel seemed quite upset,' Neal probed as he caught up with the nurse. 'She seemed to think she has been raped here, and that she is pregnant.'

Davies jerked his head towards Neal. There was anger in his eyes.

'What are you implying? That we rape our patients here? That we maltreat them?'

'No,' Neal replied, taken aback by the man's sensitivity. 'I'm merely reporting what she said. I have to add that she did seem to be lactating—'

'Listen you, you're the psychiatrist. She is taking big doses of chlorpromazine which is causing her to lactate.' He sniffed. 'You're the one who's supposed to know that chlorpromazine stimulates the release of prolactin from the pituitary,' he continued sarcastically. 'So she thinks this means she is pregnant, and that we rape her. She is sick.'

Neal nodded. He struggled to contain his mounting anger, but conceded to himself that the man was probably right. Chlorpromazine did indeed have this side effect, and this could explain her delusional system. He let the insulting tone pass. There were more important things at stake.

They entered the ward with its rows of beds crammed along opposing walls. It was bedtime, for the patients were tucked in, rolling around under the covers in an attempt to find a comfortable position. Heads turned as the two figures entered the ward. Someone hurled abuse at them.

This is really like Bedlam, Neal thought. Perhaps that is why such an unlikely man is in charge.

Miriam Umbuti was at the far end of the ward. When the two men drew up alongside her bed, she tried to sit up, but only managed to get her head momentarily off the pillow before it rolled back. She glanced with terror at the nursing officer, and then quickly averted her gaze.

'Please be brief,' Davies asked, but the tone was not requesting.

'Miriam, I am Dr Potter,' Neal began. 'I have come to see you from Wellington Hospital where you were before. How are you feeling?'

Miriam shook her head, but could not summon a reply.

'Are you happy here?'

There was a pause, and another furtive glance in the

nursing officer's direction. Then with what seemed a super-human effort, she pushed herself towards Neal.

'No, Doctor! Take me away. They—' she started, but the cough from Davies cut her short. She shook her head again.

'They?' Neal persisted.

Nothing.

'Can I speak to her alone for a minute?' Neal turned to the nurse.

'I'm afraid not.' Davies pushed his hands into the pockets of his white coat. 'I have to take responsibility for these patients, and you have given me no proof you are a doctor. No, I must stay.'

It was no use. Neal turned back to Miriam.

'Do you know where you are now?' Neal began, to probe her mental state.

She nodded. 'Umzimkulu.'

'Can you remember how long you have been here?'

'A month. A month or two. No. I'm not sure.' She closed her eyes.

'Do you know why you are here?'

She shook her head this time, still keeping her eyes closed.

'Miriam, do you think that anything strange is going on in this place?'

Neal could see the nursing officer shoot him an angry glance, but it was a routine question designed to elicit paranoia. There was a long pause before Miriam Umbuti finally opened her eyes, shaking her head pathetically.

'Time to go, man. We don't want to disturb the patients too much.'

Neal glanced at the nursing officer. He wanted to ask Miriam more, but he reckoned it would need an official form shoved under the nursing officer's nose.

He decided it was time to leave, and turned to follow the man out. When they passed the nursing office, Davies asked Neal to wait for him to lock it. While Davies fingered through his many keys, Neal studied the contents of the office. There were rows of bottles containing drugs, a large cabinet, a desk, and a chair. Unremarkable.

Except for a row of red glow-worms on the window-sill.

Neal looked again. It was a rack of blood samples, glowing as the late afternoon sun streamed in through the tall windows. It was a challenge.

That was when he knew he would have to come back.

'We've had a visitor,' Davies began.

He twisted round in his swivel chair while he listened, almost tangling himself with the phone cord. After one revolution he sat up sharply.

'You've never said we should prevent anyone coming around . . .' he spluttered.

Pause.

'A Dr Potter, I think.'

Davies had to hold the receiver away from his ear.

'OK, OK, I get the message. No more snoopers. And if Potter comes around again, make sure he doesn't leave.'

Davies put down the phone. He hated being shouted at. But there were compensations.

Those were the instructions he liked.

Neal parked the Fiat out of sight under the flat-topped thorn trees and made his way back to the asylum on foot.

Using the shield of the long grass outside the fence, he studied the terrain. From this vantage-point, it was obvious that the Rehabilitation Unit was built on a small hill, with the chapel at the top and the other four buildings on the slopes. He could only see the main building on the slope facing him, which meant that he was only visible from that building.

It did not take long to find the blind spot. At the opposite end of the building facing him was what looked like a tool shed. If he approached it squarely, he would not be visible from any of the large windows on that side of the ward.

Neal was soon tracing his way around the fence, ducking underneath, carefully avoiding the barbs, and running doubled over towards the shed. Running in that way up a hill made him breathless. Either that or he was unfit. Or scared.

He waited with his back against the wooden shed and let his pulse rate drop below eighty. His excitement put paid to any ideas of it slowing any further. Still, high cardiac outputs could be useful in emergencies.

He glanced down the front of the building. It was clear.

Keeping close to the wall, he crawled slowly along the gutter. Although the windows were ceiling-to-floor, the ward was built on raised foundations, and this meant he was concealed from view.

When he reached the steps leading up to the entrance, he paused and listened. It was deathly quiet apart from the Piet-my-vrou calling to his mate in the distance. For some reason the crickets were silent.

Skirting the steps at a run, Neal was soon hugging the building again, counting the windows. When he had counted five, he stopped. He checked his pulse. One hundred. And rising. He was not made for this sort of work, he decided. His stomach ached, his palms and soles were soaked, his head throbbed, and his hands shook.

He rehearsed the plan. It would be impossible if Davies was in the office, and it could get nasty if he was seen. Perhaps he could say he had come back for his dark glasses?

Neal shook his head, not really believing that Davies was a man with whom one could reason. No, if he was spotted, he was going to have to make a run for it.

He also knew if he delayed any longer, his nerve would give out. He straightened himself slowly, keeping his head to the side of the wall and away from what he had calculated to be the nursing office window. So far so good. Then he leaned forward slightly, giving himself a small angle to look into the office.

There was no Davies. That was the good news. But the blood samples on the sill had gone.

Neal bit his lip, flattening himself against the wall once more. He had not considered that possibility. A brief check confirmed that he had the right window. It was the nursing office, all right. But no tubes on the sill.

'Shit!' Neal cursed under his breath.

He moved towards the edge of the window and had a good look inside. After a thorough search, he spotted them in the corner on the filing cabinet. Well out of reach.

Growing more confident now, he stayed at the pane, giving himself enough time to study the ward which he could see through the nursing observation window. The patients were all in bed, presumably heavily sedated to give the nurse an easy time. There was no sign of Davies.

'Now go!'

He tried the window. Nothing. He shoved again, this time putting his weight behind it.

It rattled suddenly upwards, startling Neal more than anyone else. He blew out the air from his lungs in a quiet hissing sound, not knowing whether to be pleased or disappointed. Either way, he could not turn back.

Before he began pulling himself through the window, he quietly moved aside the bottles of drugs on the sill, noting the labels. Some contained standard drugs like chlorpromazine, others volatile anæsthetic agents like Ether, Halothane and Cyclopropane.

He frowned. There was no time to think about what they were doing there.

He hauled himself up, swinging one leg over the edge. It was when he was astride the window that he heard them.

Footsteps coming up the corridor.

Neal froze for a moment, caught on the ledge, undecided which leg to follow. It was not the time to carry on a long, internal debate. The footsteps were growing louder.

Probably Davies. Probably about to come into the office. Probably would see the open window. That would be it. Neal's numbed brain crunched out its conclusion. There was no choice. He had to hope that Davies was not coming into the office.

He swung his leg over too hurriedly, in the process knocking over a bottle of ether. It teetered for what seemed like minutes on the windowsill before tumbling in slow motion towards the floor.

It was as if Neal was watching himself in a movie. From his crouched position under the window, he saw the bottle tumble, saw himself turn reflexly and throw himself underneath it. Then he watched it smack into his sternum. Safe.

He scrambled up and wedged himself behind the door, struggling to hold down his panting respiration, feeling as if his heart would break through his chest wall.

The footsteps grew louder, slowed, and stopped at the office door. There was a pause. Then the footsteps started to move away.

Neal was about to breathe out a controlled sigh of relief when he heard the footsteps pause, and then return. Then the horrible sound of rattling keys penetrated into the nursing office.

There was no return. No reasoning.

Davies opened the door and walked to the desk. He set down the notes he was carrying, pulled out his chair, and sat himself down. There was obviously some paperwork to be done.

If Davies had turned his head, there would have been no way Neal would have been missed. Although the door was open, it was not open wide enough to afford him any cover. And then there was the obvious fact that sometime Davies would have to leave.

Neal took a deep breath and pulled off the rubber lid from the bottle of volatile anæsthetic liquid with a loud plop. As Davies jumped in his chair and turned his startled face towards the door, Neal flung the contents at him.

The colourless liquid splashed into his face, spilled down on to his chest, and soaked into his khaki shirt and white coat.

The element of surprise gave Neal valuable seconds. As Davies spluttered and rubbed his eyes, Neal grabbed the door, swung himself around, and dived out of the office. He hoped it would not be long.

Davies lunged blindly after him, snatching at his shirt,

and pulling it free. But it slipped through his wet fingers, leaving Neal unfettered.

Neal stormed down the corridor with the bull-necked charge nurse in hot pursuit, the hospital booming with their footsteps and rasping respiration. Fitness and strength were telling, and foot by foot Davies narrowed the gap. Would it work?

Grabbing a pillar, Neal swung himself down the central wing, fear now doing most of the running. He was panicking —the thought of a physical encounter with Davies was not appealing.

Then the footsteps behind him became uneven, and he turned to see Davies stagger in a stuporose state, totter, and collapse. The ether which had soaked into his clothes had found its way into his lungs, into his blood, into his brain. He was anæsthetized.

Neal let his tired legs slow down. They had earned a rest. Standing over Davies, he knew he had a few minutes while the liquid that was soaked into his clothes vapourized and kept him under.

Time enough to collect a sample or two of blood.

CHAPTER 15

Jill sat back in her chair and looked out of the window dreamily. Her heart was not exactly in her work. Instead, thoughts about the previous evening were occupying her attention.

'I think you just might be in love!' she told herself, toying with a loose lock of her blonde hair.

Her reverie was interrupted by the sister reminding her that she still had patients to see. It was Friday afternoon and Dr Peters's white infertility clinic. Not as busy as the black clinic. But the weekend was too close to allow her to concentrate.

The clinic sister ushered in a couple in their mid-thirties.

They were obviously nervous, and their forced smiles stopped at their exposed teeth. Jill glanced down at the folder in front of her, confirming they were Dr and Mrs du Toit.

Jill presumed he was a doctor of philosophy from the way he was dressed. The worn tweed jacket hung awkwardly on his bony frame, and the stretched pockets looked as though they had been frequently distorted by nervous fists while lecturing. He was extending his hand, and the cold, moist handshake confirmed her picture.

The wife looked like a mirror image. She was plump and, though nervous, was more at ease than her awkward husband. Jill extended her hand to the wife, and ushered them into the seats in front of her desk. Then she opened the folder, taking up her pen.

'Dr and Mrs du Toit?'

They nodded.

'Could you tell me what the problem is?'

The husband looked towards his wife, and she took up the cue.

'Um. When we started to try for a family, a routine pap smear revealed invasive cervical carcinoma. I had a hysterectomy.'

Jill gulped audibly. Mrs du Toit paused, unsure of how to proceed.

'I'm sorry, Mrs du Toit—' Jill looked up from her notes —'but did I understand you correctly? Did you have a total hysterectomy rather than a minor cauterization?'

'That is right, Doctor.'

'I'm not sure if there has been a mistake,' Jill began. 'Unfortunately we are not able to help couples where the wife has had a hysterectomy. You see, the uterus is fairly basic equipment . . .' Jill trailed off, not knowing how to soften the blow.

The couple looked stunned. It was the husband who finally broke the silence.

'There must be some mistake,' he said desperately. 'We were told that something could be done . . .'

'Have you thought of adoption?' Jill tried to sound positive.

'We thought of it—' Mrs du Toit took up the question— 'but then we . . .'

She did not finish her sentence. The door burst open and Peters strode into the room.

'Dr Bates, did you not read the referral letter?' he blurted.

Jill started. She was not used to her boss being so aggressive, especially in front of patients. She glanced down at the list, and saw with embarrassment that she was due to see another couple.

'I'm sorry, Dr Peters.' She looked up. 'I just didn't check the folder with my list. I see I'm due to see someone else.'

'Right.' Peters kept himself in check. He swung round and faced the couple sitting awkwardly in their seats, looking away. Like ostriches trying to make the problem disappear.

Peters tried a sweeter tone, but he sounded sarcastic. 'I'm so sorry for this inconvenience, Dr and Mrs du Toit. I'm Dr Peters. Your GP wrote to me about you. Would you mind coming into my office?'

Without another glance in Jill's direction, Peters walked out of her clinic room, followed by the du Toits who smiled weakly once more in Jill's direction.

'What the hell did I do to deserve that?' Jill wondered.

It was unlike Peters to be so rude. He was normally very courteous and well-behaved, especially in front of his patients. In fact he made it part of his teaching to instruct his students how to relate to patients. He had certainly broken his rules on this occasion.

'What's so wrong with seeing a different couple anyway?' she demanded aloud. 'What's so special about the bloody du Toits?'

The clinic sister popped her embarrassed face round the still open door. 'Gosh, I'm sorry, love. I really should have made sure you had the right patients. But I didn't anticipate that, did you?'

Jill shook her head. 'It's OK, Sister. You're forgiven, if

you can get me a cup of tea before my next patient. I need it.'

The nurse's face beamed. 'You're on. And at least I can bring you some good news. Your last couple have cancelled.'

'That *is* good news. I've had enough for one week.'

While the two women had tea in the staff room, Jill asked the sister: 'What do you think is eating Dr Peters? It's not like him to lose his cool.'

'Don't know, love.' The sister looked up from her cup of tea. 'I think it must be the hospital cuts. Only this morning he was saying that he wouldn't be surprised if the next Government directive to the hospital would be that all black women should have hysterectomies. Carrying on, he was. In quite a state. Saying that what the Afrikaners wanted to do was to get blacks to stop reproducing.'

Jill jumped. *What the Afrikaners wanted to do was to get blacks to stop reproducing.* It was exactly what she had jokingly said to Neal might be happening. It was exactly how she had explained the unusual post-partum cases.

She caught the nursing sister looking at her closely.

'You all right, love?'

Jill pulled herself up. 'Fine, Sister. Just tired, that's all. It's been a long day, and I still have some letters to dictate.'

Jill made her way back to her room, and began scraping around for a spare tape for dictation. For the second time that day she was interrupted. But this time there was a knock at the door.

'Come in!' she called out, still rummaging.

It was Peters. Jill flinched involuntarily, anticipating a second tirade.

'I'm sorry for barging in on you like that, Jill,' Peters offered. 'Unforgivable, really. It was just that I had promised the GP that I'd see the couple myself. And I guess it's the end of a long and difficult day . . .'

Jill nodded in acceptance and changed the subject.

'What are you going to do about the clinic being closed down?'

'Well, I'm certainly not going to roll over and die, I can

assure you. We must certainly be seen to be closing the black infertility clinic down, and that is precisely what we will do. We will start to accept fewer and fewer patients until eventually the whole clinic will fold.'

Then Peters struck the table with his fist, grinning mischievously across at Jill.

'But what I'll do is absorb all these patients into my endocrine clinic. If these racists think that I am going to join their campaign to reduce the black population, they have no conception—excuse the pun—of what they will be up against.'

Peters laughed, strutting to the door. He paused.

'Listen. Sorry again about the outburst. OK?' With that, he was gone.

Maybe there really was a plot afoot to reduce black numbers. Maybe she was right. Maybe Peters was right.

Jill headed for Brandsma's secretary to pick up a tape for dictation. Professor Brandsma's office was on the top floor of the building with a spectacular view of the Durban coastline. When she walked in, the secretary was busy.

She was the sort of woman Jill felt gave femininity a bad name. Her hair was died platinum blonde, and she spoke in a high-pitched whine like a spoilt child. She had a curious blind spot for other women, while men were noticed all too readily. So when Jill stood in front of her desk, she had to ask repeatedly before she obtained a response.

'I'm sorry, Dr Bates, but your dictaphone has not been fixed. You'll have to use it without the fast-forward or fast-reverse.'

The secretary turned back to her work with a dismissive flick of the head. The conversation was over. Jill grabbed the machine, picked up a tape from the typing pool, and stormed out of the office. She nearly bumped into Professor Brandsma.

'Professor, may I have a word?' she found herself saying.

'Can't it wait? I have an appointment in five minutes.' His voice was gruff, almost rude.

'No, sir, it can't, but I won't keep you long.'

Brandsma paused, studying her closely. Then he led the way into his office, and without offering Jill a chair, seated himself at his desk.

'Professor. I think something interesting is emerging from the trial.'

Brandsma's eyelids rose sceptically.

'There is a large number of women who are becoming psychotic immediately post-partum . . .'

Jill stopped. She had been studying his face carefully, looking for any flicker of concern, any twitch of anxiety. And something had registered there.

'Ach, Dr Bates. You exaggerate. Do you know how many babies we deliver in Wellington a year?'

Jill shook her head.

'Well, it is over ten thousand.' Brandsma paused in mid-flight, his voice becoming more aggressive as he continued. 'And do you know the incidence of post-partum psychosis in the general population?'

Again Jill shook her head.

'One to two per thousand births.' Brandsma stood up and went to the window to look out. 'Now tell me how many cases of post-partum psychosis you have found in the trial?'

'Eighteen.'

With that Brandsma swung on her.

'Right, Dr Bates. If you have any mathematical ability at all, you will see that the incidence in my cases is no higher than in the general population.' He came round from the window to tower over her. 'Now if you will excuse me . . .'

Jill got the message. Brandsma was usually difficult to deal with, rude, aggressive, sarcastic. But there had been fear in his eyes at the mention of the post-partum psychotics.

And wasn't there something wrong with his arithmetic?

Davies was still groggy when he made the call.

'Boss, I'm afraid I just can't remember what happened in between. I came back to the office, to write some notes, I think, and then the next thing I remember is that I'm lying in the middle of the corridor soaked in bloody ether.'

Davies stretched himself and yawned involuntarily as he listened.

'No, I don't think it was Potter—he'd already gone.'

Davies looked at the broken bottle of ether underneath the window which was slightly ajar.

'What's that?'

Pause.

'Ja. But I don't know anything about this post-anæsthetic retrograde amnesia you're talking about. All I know is that I can't remember what happened . . .'

But he was beginning to think. 'I got an idea. Maybe I left the window open, so as when I come in, the curtain blows over a bottle of gas. I try to catch it, maybe. But it breaks, splashing over me . . .'

Another pause.

'Ja. I know. You do the thinking.'

Davies pulled a face while he listened.

'No. Don't worry. There's nothing missing.'

All doctors were the same, he decided as he listened to the irritated voice on the phone.

'OK, OK. It could have been Potter coming back to snoop around. But don't worry. I haven't forgotten—my memory's not that bad. If he comes back, he leaves feet first.'

'Don't you ever take a break?'

Neal was amazed to find McKenzie still working at the laboratory. But delighted.

'Nappies have to be bought.' McKenzie looked up from the centrifuge and grinned. 'Got that LSD sample for me yet?'

'Damn!' Neal cursed. 'I left some vials in my office. I'll get them in a sec. But I have some samples for you. If you're able. And willing.'

'An epidemic of LSD. I can just see it,' McKenzie joked. 'Be a good title for the *British Medical Journal*.'

'I see you're sceptical?'

'Hmm.' McKenzie finished loading the centrifuge and switched it on. 'Scepticism is the scientist's way of life. It all sounds too extraordinary, doesn't it? An LSD party?'

Neal shrugged.

'But don't worry,' McKenzie continued. 'I'll run the test. Just don't expect any answers, OK?'

CHAPTER 16

Jill arrived at her office deep in thought. When she had first suggested to Neal that Brandsma might be driving his obstetric patients mad, it had been little more than a joke.

Yes, she had considered him capable of doing something like that. But she hadn't seriously thought he was actually doing it.

Not, that is, until now.

Jill could feel her heart race, and her thoughts were keeping up. Was Brandsma's obesity trial just one big smokescreen? Was the Afrikaner really abusing his position to further his political ends? And how was he doing it? She had seen no obvious foul play.

With an effort, she pulled her runaway mind into line, settling at her desk with her dictaphone. When she had her first folder open, she noticed that the tape was not wound to the end. She cursed the secretary for being slow to send her machine to repairs, resigning herself to listening to the tail-end of someone else's summary.

While the tape droned in the background, she tried to relax. The name 'Umzimkulu Rehabilitation Unit' jolted her attention back to her worries.

She stopped the tape, and ran it back. Then she started it again.

'The patient was discharged on ferrous sulphate 300 milligrams daily,' the voice dictated, 'and was followed up by the district nurse. End of summary.'

Then the voice changed.

'This is Mrs King. I . . . um . . . we saw you yesterday in the Obstetric Department about our child due soon. And we just wanted to be sure that we are to come to the Umzimkulu Rehabilitation Unit on Wednesday the 27th. If we don't hear from you, we will see you then. Goodbye.'

There followed a loud bleep, a crackle, and then the tape whined on to the end.

Jill frowned. The recording was certainly not a summary.

'Sounds more like a tape-recording of a telephone conversation,' she thought aloud.

Then the penny dropped. 'It *is* a telephone conversation,' she said aloud to herself with excitement. 'It's a recorded telephone message.'

Somehow a tape from a recording machine had got mixed up in the typing pool.

Her suspicions resurfaced. What was the connection between some expectant mother and a lunatic asylum? Was Brandsma running a concentration camp there, keeping black women from reproducing further?

She shuddered.

'God! I have to find Neal,' she told herself, reluctant to pursue such a matter further on her own.

Leaving her office, she made her way down to the basement towards the lift that would take her to the Psychiatry Department. When she was about to step into the connecting basement corridor, something instinctively held her back.

Someone was coming up the corridor. There were two of them, from the sound of it, and they were in conversation, talking softly.

Jill pressed herself against the wall and listened.

'*Kyk hier*,' one of them was saying. 'I don't want any of this getting out. I want our work to be kept absolutely secret, do you hear?'

'Yes, Professor.'

The two men walked past the entrance where Jill skulked in the shadows. It was Brandsma and Neal!

It was a terrible shock, a shock that sent a wave of heat

spreading over her body, leaving her dizzy and breathless. Neal involved in something secret with Brandsma? What the hell was going on?

'And another thing,' Brandsma's voice continued up the corridor. 'One of my registrars, Dr Bates, has been digging around. Get her off it, all right?'

'I'll see what I can do, Prof.'

Then the voices became too indistinct.

Jill slid down the wall to slump on the last step. If her thoughts were pressured before, they were positively spinning now. So there *was* a secret. And what was it? Was it what she had jocularly suggested initially? That Brandsma had a plan to reduce black fertility? If so, how could a decent man like Neal be involved? It didn't make sense.

She resolved to go and ask Neal what was going on. There was bound to be a simple explanation. She would wait for Neal at his office until he returned from his talk with Brandsma.

But when she arrived at his office, her confidence in an easy explanation had weakened. What if Neal had been bought off?

On impulse she tried his door. It was open. Checking the corridor first, she slipped inside. The office was sparsely furnished—just a desk piled high with notes, and a chair. She didn't know exactly what she was looking for, but started with the drawers. The first was unremarkable— it was cluttered with pens, hospital request forms, and test-tubes.

The second contained a shock. It was empty apart from two vials. She nearly ignored them, taking them to be some standard psychiatric drugs. But then she decided to have a closer look.

Lysergic Acid Diethylamide.

Jill's stomach churned. What was Neal doing with LSD? Unless he was poisoning her patients?

She continued her search, frantically now, feeling suddenly claustrophobic.

Rummaging through the papers on his desk, she caught

sight of an envelope addressed to Neal in familiar hand-writing. It looked like Brandsma's. Struggling to contain her trembling fingers, feeling sick at heart, she tore it open. Her eyes opened wide, trying to take it all in. Then they squeezed shut.

In the envelope was a cheque for R1000. A cheque written out to Dr Potter. A personal cheque of Professor J. Brandsma's.

She knew then that she would have to go to the Umzimkulu Rehabilitation Unit alone.

Neal had intended doing a quick ward round before returning to the laboratory. But other things were on his mind. He bleeped Jill.

'Hallo. Dr Jill Bates here. You bleeped?'

'Hi, Jill,' Neal spoke warmly into the phone.

Silence.

'Jill! You there?'

Silence.

'Shit! Someone has cut us off. Are you still there?'

'Yes.'

This time it was Neal's turn to be silent.

'Hey! Is anything the matter?' he finally spoke up. 'You sound . . . awfully distant.'

'So would you if your best friend turned against you.'

'What do you mean?'

'Are you saying that you and Brandsma aren't up to something, trying to keep me out?'

'Good heavens, Jill! I don't know what you're talking about.'

'So you deny it, then. You deny working with Brandsma, driving women mad with LSD, being on his payroll?'

'Good God, woman! Don't get so bloody paranoid.'

As soon as he had said it, he regretted it. He had forgotten about her family history.

'You're hardly the one to judge me, Neal Potter. Don't you know that you can't judge a belief to be paranoid unless you discover it to be false?'

'Listen, Jill, I shouldn't have said—'

'No, you shouldn't. And I shan't be able to make tonight either.'

Then the line went dead.

CHAPTER 17

As the night closed in on the small Mini bumping about on the coastal road to the Umzimkulu Rehabilitation Unit, Jill wondered what it was she was going to look for. Until she asked herself some questions.

'If I wanted to keep the black population down, how would I do it? Assuming I was an obstetrician? Probably use tubal ligations. They're cheap, easy to perform, and nobody would be the wiser. Perhaps the Professor is tying Fallopian tubes in the secrecy of his mental asylum.'

With a start she realized the significance of the recorded telephone message. Brandsma was enticing his pregnant mothers there, perhaps after delivery, to ensure they did not reproduce again.

Then she knew what she had to do. She would go to the mental asylum and look for signs that such operations were being performed. There would at least be some point in the drive out there, though it was a point which was becoming less land less obvious to Jill as the journey progressed.

The moon was casting an eerie light over the countryside as she swept through the sugar cane. She could see the swell of the sea below, the waves catching the moonlight as they rose and swept into the shore. There was a stillness that was almost palpable, casting a spell on her as she tried to concentrate on the road.

The turn-off appeared as the hospital porter had instructed and Jill drove on till she drew up alongside a pair of rusty iron gates. She flicked off her headlamps and paused, allowing her eyes to build up night pigment.

Nothing was clear at first, but soon the gates defined

themselves again in the pale moonlight. Time to continue
the journey on foot.

The night air was calm but laced with a chilling edge.
Jill shivered, reaching to the back seat for her jumper.
Pulling it over her head, she flicked out her long blonde hair
before moving away from the car.

Close up, she could see that the iron gate was dilapidated
but securely locked. It looked like she was going to have to
play at being a tomboy again. When she was astride the
gate, she saw an illuminated window in the nearest building.

'Probably the nursing office,' she whispered.

Trying to keep the rashness of her nocturnal adventure
at the back of her mind, trying to keep her pulse rate down
and her breathing calm, she swung her leg over the top rail
and lowered herself to the ground.

'How am I going to explain my presence if I am caught?'
she asked herself. 'It won't look good if they really are
involved in something awful. On the other hand, if I went
in broad daylight, my cover story could be quite innocent.'

Jill hesitated. She was about to turn around and head
home when the silence of the night was splintered by a shrill
scream. This was followed by other windows flickering into
light.

'No. It's now or never.'

Gritting her teeth, she stealthily followed the drive up to
the building. When she neared the walls, she found the
windows were higher than she had expected, and she had
to stand on tiptoe to see inside.

It was a ward, with not a great deal of light apart from
a single overhead lamp above one patient's curtained bed.
Two figures were thrown on to the curtains, and as they
moved around, their shadows were distorted in the curtain
folds into hideous two-dimensional monsters. There was a
shifting form in the bed, and its muffled groans penetrated
through the window and out into the night. Now the swinging shadow of a suspended bottle could be seen reflected on
to the curtains.

Jill was not sure what was going on. Psychiatry had never

been one of her strong points, and she couldn't remember whether intravenous sedation was ever used.

She watched the two figures at the bedside. One appeared to be holding down the writhing form in the bed. The other was straightening, holding something up to the light. Probably a syringe.

The inchoate form in the bed was screaming again, writhing with more vigour, and the single shadow holding her down shuddered with her convulsions.

Perhaps she was having a fit. But no patient she knew screamed continuously during a fit.

The other shadow was bending over again, in order, Jill presumed, to administer the injection. The writhing in the bed gradually subsided, then suddenly ceased altogether. With that the two figures stood upright.

Jill frowned. Then panicked. 'God! Maybe she's dead!'

A new and more horrible possibility suggested itself to her. Perhaps Brandsma was keeping the women there till he was sure they would not be missed, and then killing them. Perhaps she should be looking for an oven rather than an operating theatre . . .

She shivered again. She would have preferred to have had a more phlegmatic imagination.

'OK, OK. Don't jump to conclusions. Just have a look around,' she told herself. 'See what you can find.'

She lowered herself out of sight. There was cramp in her foot, and she had to massage it before the muscles relaxed. Seated in the flowerbed, she took stock. The nurses would return to the nursing office. Then she could explore.

Straightening up, she moved around the building in search of an open window or door. The light from the ward illuminated the ghostly mist rolling up the hill from the sea, mist which was concealing the building ahead. With the strong smell of seaweed in her nostrils, and a palpitating sense of adventure, she hugged the wall of the building and moved slowly round.

The block was shaped like the letter T. As she moved round the side of the building, she came across the central wing. Then the light from the ward flickered off, making her pause for a moment to acclimatize her eyes once more to the dark. When they had, she moved forward again, locating a door at the junction of the central and left wings. She tried the handle, careful not to make any noise.

To her surprise, the door gave way easily, creaking a little. She stopped and waited, listening to hear whether she had betrayed her presence. There was nothing.

She moved inside the dark corridor, gently easing the door closed. Poised to study her surroundings, she heard a click. Immediately a neon strip on the ceiling flickered the corridor into light. Jill flung herself behind a nearby pillar. She hoped she was on the right side.

Two voices drifted down the corridor. She breathed out quietly. She was on the right side. The voices grew louder. Then other sounds defined themselves. There was the creaking of poorly oiled wheels, and someone moaning.

'How long do you think it'll take?'

'Don't worry, man. I am sure we will have the second payment by the morning—everything will be A-OK. You mustn't be so nervous. Did that doctor shake you up this afternoon?'

The voices were quite distinct now, and as they moved closer Jill eased herself round the back of the pillar, squeezing herself between it and the wall. She caught sight of the front of a trolley as it was wheeled noisily down the corridor. She held her breath as it passed.

'Ja. I guess it did. It's not the first time people have visited the home. It's not the first time a doctor has visited the home either. But he was from Wellington and was following up some of his patients. I think he might be on to something.'

'The patients' paranoia is rubbing off on you, my man! What did our own doc say?'

'He don't like it either. He said we got to make a plan for the man.'

'You given him a bleep?'

'Ja.'

The voices faded out of earshot. Jill began to exhale, but as she did so, she could feel the beginning of an irresistible impulse to cough which caught her too offguard to stifle.

Almost as her breath came out in a bark, she began to squeeze herself round the pillar and run for the next pillar down the corridor, hoping she would stay out of sight.

'Hey! What's that?'

'Somebody there?'

Jill barely heard. She had committed herself. She had to run. She weaved between the wall and the pillars, hardly listening for the sound of pursuing footsteps, concentrating on staying out of sight. As she got to the next pillar, the frequency of footsteps behind her moved into a higher gear. The chase was on.

It was almost by accident that she switched off the light. Slipping through the last pillar, she caught her shoulder on the switch. The old-fashioned brass knob sank into her loose-fitting sweater and tugged violently as she went by.

Jill cursed under her breath, twisting round to see what had ensnared her. With sweaty and tremulous hands, she fumbled for the offending object. She found it and pulled herself free. As she did so, she accidentally plunged the corridor back into darkness.

It took her a second to realize what she had done, and when she did she knew she had won valuable time. Slipping off her shoes, she headed across the hall to the other wing. She was going to give the nurses a run-around.

As she ran down the corridor as quietly she could, she widened her eyes in an attempt to soak in any available light, readying her hands to break a fall. Most of the illumination was coming from the moonlight filtering through a window at the far end of the corridor, and for Jill it was the light at the end of the tunnel.

She reached the entrance to the ward just as a lightening flicker began behind her. She flung herself behind the door, hoping that her pursuer was looking in the opposite direction.

She looked frantically about. She was in another ward. What to do now?

Time was ticking away and it wouldn't take the nurses long before they realized they had the wrong ward. She sneaked a look down the corridor. A short stocky man in a white coat was emerging from the opposite ward and running up the hall. Jill could feel the panic tighten in her stomach. She turned to face the ward, desperately scratching around for something to do. Someone in the ward stirred and cried out in her sleep.

Before she had time to think the idea through, Jill ululated at the top of her voice, and bounded to the nearest patient, pulling the covers off and jolting her rudely out of bed.

She stormed down the ward, moving from bed to bed, wreaking havoc as she went. Startled patients plummeted out of bed on to the floor, and hearing the infectious war-cry, began to move into the centre of the ward and join in the ululation. Stuporose forms staggered about the ward, calling upon their imaginary menfolk to take up arms, and belligerently bumping other patients out of the way.

Jill thankfully dived under the bed at the far end of the ward and concentrated on taking deep breaths. No mistakes this time. She had done all she could. Now she had to wait.

The ward light went on. The night nurse had arrived.

'Jesus H. Christ! What the hell is going on here?'

The nurse stood immobile at the entrance of the ward surveying the scene. Then Jill watched as he began the laborious task of getting the patients back to their beds. She could see the heavy leather boots mingle with the black feet of the patients, and the strange four-legged beast stagger backwards and forwards. Inch by inch, the beast was getting nearer.

'What's going on?' Reinforcements had arrived.

'Not sure. I think we had another sleepwalker.'

'A sleepwalker that switches off corridor lights?'

'OK, OK. Some of these patients are hardly getting sedation now. It's too close to the end.'

'Well, I'm going to let the bull-mastiffs out anyway. I
don't like the idea of a snooper, not at this stage. No, man!'

The second nurse left the ward. It was settling quickly, the
patients responding to the authoritative bark of the nurse.

With the way they sound, they hardly need dogs, Jill
thought.

The boots were quite close now, and Jill squeezed herself
into a ball and waited. The ululation in the ward had
stopped, and the grunting of the nurse and the occasional
cry was all that disturbed the once noisy ward. She watched
the boots and the bare feet of the last patient dance strange
steps towards the bed. Then the bed creaked and sagged on
to her.

'Right. That's that. I wonder which of you crazies was
wandering out there in the corridor? Huh?'

The boots remained by the bedside, and for one terrible
moment Jill thought the man knew she was there and was
simply prolonging her agony. She waited for the upturned
smirking face staring at her from the edge of the bed. It did
not appear.

The boots turned and moved off up the corridor, stopping
once to survey a much quieter ward before disappearing out
of sight. Then the lights went out.

The first round had been won, and that was something
to be grateful for. But there were no doubt more to come.
And there were the dogs.

She was trapped, and she knew it. There was no way she
was going to set foot in the grounds to lock jaws with a
bull-mastiff. Bull-mastiffs were not the sort of friendly pet
one would get for one's children. They had been artificially
selected over generations for their viciousness, honed into
killing machines. Jill was not about to be their next victim.

The alternative was not appetizing either. It meant she
would have to stay in the hospital grounds till morning,
perhaps even till the next evening. Her heart sank.

Maybe she should give herself up?

Bits of conversation drifted back into her mind, and she
soon realized that this was not an option. The more she

learned about things, the more convinced she was that something sinister was going on, and her presence wouldn't be treated kindly.

Why should they bother with dogs if there was nothing to hide? What was so terrible about an intruder in a mental hospital, unless there was something to conceal?

Jill screwed up her face.

One of them had been worried that the visiting doctor had been 'on to something'. What could that mean unless there was something they didn't want uncovered?

Whatever it all meant, Jill knew she had to stay in the asylum till morning.

'And if I have to stay, I'm going to stay and find out,' she said grimly.

CHAPTER 18

Neal had had enough. His ward round would have to wait. Perhaps McKenzie had something to cheer him up. Not forgetting the vials of LSD, he headed for the laboratory. When he got there, McKenzie was bending over the electrophoresis tray.

'Thanks for the LSD. But we can't calibrate just yet—the mass spectrometer is in repairs. Hence the electrophoresis. It'll take about an hour. Care for some supper?' McKenzie closed his notes. He looked tired.

'Sure. Listen, after that run, let's call it a day, huh?' Neal clapped his friend on the back.

McKenzie looked up and smiled weakly. 'It's that obvious, is it?'

Neal nodded. 'Listen, man, I'll buy you some nappies if you like. Just promise me you'll get some sleep.'

McKenzie laughed, pushing himself to his feet. 'I promise! Should we try canteen food?'

'Now I know you are really tired. The dinners should carry a biohazard warning.'

McKenzie chuckled again. He was reviving. 'It's fish and chips, then?'

Neal nodded. The local seafront café was infinitely preferable. The food was tasty, there was the fresh sea breeze, the calming view of the sea, and they could leave the museum of the sick behind.

They took their fish and chips, wrapped in newspaper, and ate them on the rocks, watching the waves roll in, trying to forget the ugly building looming behind them. The sun was a fiery red ball burning just above the ocean, throwing a warm glow on the surrounding sky, mesmerizing them. There were children running about on the beach, teasing the waves, tempting the onrushing water to catch them.

But try as he might, Neal could not relax. There was something on his mind. After he had wolfed down his food, he told McKenzie he would meet him back in the laboratory in an hour. He had a date with the computer.

The admissions officer was thankfully not busy when Neal arrived at Reception. There was no card game going, there were no new admissions to clerk in, and he was keen for something to do.

'I can find you anyone, man. No sweat. Just give me the name, or date of birth. No matter the hospital, no matter the illness. You name it, I can tap it,' the admissions officer quipped.

'Thanks, but there's a wee problem. I only have the surname. At least, I think I have the surname. Bates. Admitted to Constantia Asylum. She must have been born around 1940. I'm afraid that's all I have. Would you have a go?' Neal asked hopefully.

'Sure, man. No probs.'

Neal had been worrying about Jill. The more he had thought about their last conversation, the more he felt that she had sounded out of character. Too sensitive. Even paranoid.

The admissions officer swung round in his swivel chair and punched out the request on the keyboard of his computer. The green and black monitor registered 'Constantia

Asylum, Bates, d.o.b. 1941?', and the cursor flashed while
the computer searched its memory. In half a minute the
cursor moved to the next line and typed out six names.

'There you are, man. You pays your money, you takes
your pick.'

'Let's try those two, shall we?' Neal suggested. 'I don't
reckon she would have been called Arthur, James, Nathan,
or Christopher, do you?'

The admissions officer laughed. 'Right on, man. Far out!'

Armed with the two folder numbers, the admissions officer asked the computer for the diagnoses. The first woman
had had diverticulosis, agoraphobia, and a stroke. They
moved on to the second, and this too looked like a dead end.
The diagnoses of appendicitis and pneumonia flashed on
the screen before the words 'paranoid schizophrenia' were
typed.

Neal breathed a sigh of relief. 'Lucky her aunt was
paternal, and not married. Are you able to gain access to
her notes?'

'Hey, man! What about confidentiality? You've got to
have a special code for that.' The admissions officer shook
his head and clicked his tongue.

Neal slumped, and stared vacantly at the green monitor.
It was a dead end.

'Stay cool, man. Stay cool. I forgot to tell you, I just
happen to know what it is. If you are quick about it, I can
give you a peek.' The officer grinned.

Neal was relieved enough to forget about the dangers of
an admissions clerk having access to such highly confidential
and potentially explosive information. He asked for a peek.

As the admissions officer punched in the request, Neal
wondered whether the history would give him some idea of
whether Jill was becoming ill.

It was soon on the screen, and Neal leaned over the desk
to read:

Dorothy Bates is a 30-year-old woman who was well until
a week before admission. She then began to suspect the

man she had been seeing for the last year was plotting against her, planning to marry her, poison her, and thereby inherit her estate. She soon began to believe her whole family was involved. She began to sleep poorly and neglect her personal hygiene. She bought extra padlocks for her doors, and neighbours noticed her wandering round the perimeter of her house, shouting at imaginary people. On the day of admission she attacked her boy-friend at her gate, injuring him, though not seriously. She was restrained by passers-by, and taken eventually by the police to casualty.

Neal raised his eyebrows. It didn't bear thinking about. Then he remembered something else. 'Can you retrieve a list of all our current staff on that thing?'

'Your wish is my command. You want doctors, nurses, orderlies or what, man?'

'Nurses.'

Neal watched as the admission officer punched in 'Staff 1988, Nurses' and a list of names came up on the screen. He looked for a male nurse by the name of Smith.

There was none. Male or female. The call to help the escaped patient in the boiler room had been a complete fiction. A set-up.

Although Neal had no idea what was going on, he was too tired to speculate. It made more sense to wait till he had the results of the electrophoresis. There would be ample time to piece it all together then.

Neal took the external route back to the laboratory. More fresh air was needed. As he passed the front of the hospital, he caught sight once again of a figure in traditional Zulu dress. It was silhouetted by the fading sun, dancing on the rocks, waving an assegai, the short stabbing spear of the Zulu warrior, and all the while emitting a compelling rhythmic chant.

Neal stopped to watch, fascinated. It looked like some war dance, becoming more and more animated, more and more frenzied. Then, suddenly, the dance was over, the warrior staring fixedly at Wellington Hospital, his arm pulled back, ready to throw.

The assegai was unleashed, sailed through an arc, whistling as it flew, and musically embedded itself into the floor at the entrance of the hospital.

Neal ducked involuntarily. When he looked up again, the figure was gone. Puzzled, Neal checked the assegai. It was still there, vibrating, solid, dripping with fresh blood. He wasn't losing his grip on reality.

Sometimes it feels like it, he thought. He shook his head.

When he arrived back at the Chemical Pathology Laboratory, McKenzie was waiting for him at the entrance waving a long piece of paper that looked like a wet scarf. On it there were three purple ink spots.

'Any luck?' Neal managed.

'Yes!' McKenzie said excitedly.

'And?'

McKenzie stabbed at the three spots situated together in the middle of the electrophoretic paper.

'You are right, Godammit, I don't know how, but you are right. All the samples contain LSD!'

CHAPTER 19

When Neal set out to the township, it was early Saturday morning and the streets were empty except for the occasional drunk and windswept newspaper. Speedy progress was made. He had elected to wear a white coat, the badge of the white doctor. There were laws forbidding the entrance of whites into the townships, and he needed a plausible excuse for his presence there in case he was intercepted by police.

There were also the gangs of radicalized black youth to think about, quick to spot a 'whitie' and give chase. Recently there had been some awful cases of whites being 'necklaced' in the township. He hoped that his white coat would give him some immunity.

With the map of Durban district covering the steering-wheel, Neal chartered the course to Chaka Road. When the route was clear, he examined the facts once again.

The Prostitution theory had to go—Selina Zondi for one was no prostitute. Anyway, the patients were hardly withdrawing from drugs with LSD in their veins. So what did that leave? The Long Half-life theory. 48 hours after the onset, Selina Zondi was still having visual hallucinations, and still had LSD in her blood. Now, according to Professor Evans, the half-life of normal LSD was 8 hours. So if it was normal, it ought to have been excreted. Therefore the women were not getting ordinary LSD, but rather an abnormal LSD-like molecule. It had been shown to be abnormal, thanks to Mark's re-calibration of the mass spectrometer that morning. If it was more difficult for the body to eliminate, it would make the hallucinations persist. The women might all be getting some natural source of the molecule, perhaps as some herbal medicine for labour pains, making them psychotic. Hence the need to collect some samples today.

Neal eased his green Fiat on to the highway.

But a more sinister theory had also to be considered. As soon as he had stumbled on these cases, Brandsma and Isaacs had become alarmed and had begun acting suspiciously. In fact, when he had approached Brandsma to sound him out, telling him that he was interested in post-partum psychosis and wanted to do some research, the Professor became extremely nervous. And then Neal's life had suddenly become cheap. He had been lured to the boiler room on some pretext and narrowly escaped death. So perhaps Jill was right: some plot was afoot . . .

Neal's thoughts turned to Jill. He had gone round to her flat the previous night, but she had been out. He had waited there for hours, falling asleep in the Fiat, but she had not come home. Eventually he had returned to a more comfortable bed. He would have to find her later.

He wondered whether he was acting like an inexperienced psychiatrist who was seeing psychosis everywhere.

'You have doctoritis!' he accused himself. 'You learn about a disease, and then you diagnose it everywhere!'

The traffic on the highway was starting to thicken, and he had to concentrate on more practical matters. Then he spotted the turn-off to the township.

Neal turned off the highway and was soon jolting on the potholed Umfulosi road. It snaked its way up the rolling hills outside the city of Durban, wound dangerously close to the edge of the rocky cliffs, before threading through fields of sugar cane towards a city of shanties.

When he arrived at the township, blacks were filtering out on their way to work. Some were obviously dressed for a visit to the city, the men in their baggy dark pants, polished white shoes, loose-fitting cotton jackets, and the women in bright, tightly clinging dresses. Western styles had been absorbed and transformed to yield a unique African style.

The crowds stared at Neal with indifference. Doctors were frequent visitors to the white clinic there, and were tolerated. Although much needed, there was no open-armed welcome.

Chaka Road came up predictably, and he was soon alongside No. 24. It was a primitive-looking house, but at least it had a permanent feel, unlike many of the tin shanties he had encountered at the outskirts of the township. It was made of unplastered red brick and boasted a corrugated iron roof.

He climbed out of the Fiat and walked up the short path to the door. A young black boy was playing in the garden with a wire motor-car which he was pushing along with an elongated steering-wheel. It had been constructed carefully out of a single length of wire fencing with wheels cut from an old car tyre. Neal marvelled at the handiwork: no sophisticated Western toy would have provided as much pleasure.

Catching sight of him as he came up the steps, the picanin ducked inside, calling out in excitement. He waited at the door without knocking, and was soon greeted by old man Cedric Zondi.

When the old man recognized him, his face fell.

'Your granddaughter is all right, Mr Zondi. Please do not worry on that score.' Neal smiled reassuringly. 'I have just come to ask you some routine questions I neglected to ask a few days ago.'

Alarm was replaced by perplexity on the old man's face.

Neal tried to clarify. 'It's about what Selina might have taken, making her ill. Can I come inside and talk?'

The old man nodded, turned, and led the way through his dark house to the back. He had been sitting on the back veranda, and offered his guest a seat as he returned to his. The small boy seated himself at his great-grandfather's foot and stared wide-eyed at the visitor.

'I think that Selina might have been taking some herbal medicine for her early labour pains, perhaps provided by yourself or the witch doctor, before she came to hospital.'

He left the question as a statement, and watched the old man closely. He could see him react as he spoke, his dark eyes suddenly narrowing.

'I think the medicine might be responsible for her illness.'

'Ai! ai! ai!' Cedric shook his head and looked at the white-coated man facing him on the veranda. Then his gaze went through him. He was making up his mind.

'The medicine man gave Selina a special herb when she began to have the stomach cramps,' Cedric began after a pause. 'We all thought that after Gordon had died the witch doctor would forgive, and help us expel the evil spirit. But the medicine he gave did not seem to help.'

The old man paused, shaking his head as if to berate himself once more.

'Then I wondered whether the witch doctor was not using his full powers to rid us of the tokolosh. He had already used them to kill Gordon, and I thought Selina was next. So I sent her to you, thinking you could help. But now I am not sure any more . . .' his voice trailed off.

'Why is that?'

'Too many women have become possessed in your white hospital. The witch doctor told me, warned me. He said you were not there to help but to encourage the tokolosh to take possession of the women, of my Selina. Now you come to tell me you want to help. Who am I to believe?'

'Listen, Mr Zondi, if we were driving your granddaughter mad, would I come here to ask for your help in curing her? Of course not. Now I don't know what has given her this possession, but I do know that we are desperately trying to help her. And I do know that having a look at that medicine will help.'

Cedric scratched his chin. He hadn't been listening to the words, but the young man's sincerity and passion had been obvious. Selina was presumably very ill, and the doctor wanted to help. Nodding his greying head, he pushed himself slowly to his feet and disappeared inside the house.

It seemed like an age before old man Zondi returned with a small box. He set it down on the table before opening it slowly. Inside were mushrooms.

'It is the prophetic mushroom. It makes great men see far ahead, and it makes lesser men free of evil spirits. It is potent black man's medicine.'

With a tremulous hand Neal took the box and quickly slipped it into his pocket. He was eager to leave, lest the old man change his mind.

'Thank you very much, Mr Zondi. I'm sure it will help.' Neal stood up.

'You beware, Doctor.' The old man's hand reached up and gripped Neal's arm with considerable force. 'Be careful that the medicine does not fall into evil hands. For what can expel the tokolosh in good hands, in the wrong hands can invite him back in.'

Neal wasn't listening. He was trying to remember the name of the hallucinogen that comes from a mushroom. Did he have some in his hand?

CHAPTER 20

Psylocibin, he remembered once he had driven off from the house. Perhaps McKenzie's machine hadn't been programmed for it, and mistook its similar structure for LSD. Perhaps psylocibin intoxication was mimicking the post-partum psychoses.

He left Cedric Zondi's house greatly encouraged, and proceeded to visit Rachel Dlamini's home. But when he found the address, he was greeted by blank expressions. No one there had ever heard of Rachel Dlamini, or any woman fitting her description.

'I'm sorry, my baas,' the old woman who lived there said. 'We have lived here for two generations. We know no Dlamini woman.' And then the door had been closed on him.

Eventually he decided to visit the witch doctor. If anyone had a good source of unusual medicaments and was distributing hallucinogenic compounds, he was the man.

As he neared the market place, the home of the medicine man, he began to get cold feet. What would he say? Would he say he suspected him of driving women mad? That he wanted a sample of his medicines to test this hypothesis out?

I'll think of something, he thought optimistically.

The market place was alive with shouting and bargaining. Women stood in front of the stalls, jockeying for position, trying to shout one another down. The men stood at a suitable distance, discussing business, staying clear of the shopping. There was one mother sticking her tongue into the eye of her child, no doubt licking out some offending particle. A group of men were playing some form of checkers with white and black painted stones on the ground. In one corner a group of youths played kwela music, with its irresistible beat, on reed instruments. Other children danced around with the sort of grace and rhythm that characterizes the Zulu people.

Neal smiled. It was a wonderful place.

He struggled through the noisy throng and burst through to a vacant space. It was there that he almost turned back.

Directly in front of him, adorned with a wonderful necklace of the oddest assortment of dried organic appendages he had ever seen, was the medicine man—and it was the Zulu he had seen at the hospital. He could not be sure, of course. Although he had seen him on two occasions, it had been only in silhouette. Nevertheless, the poise of the man was unmistakable.

Neal froze for what seemed ages, worrying if the man would recognize him. Probably not, he eventually decided.

He watched the consultations. They were obviously public, each patient being brought by his relatives and seated on the ground opposite the medicine man. He would then listen to the relatives describe the problem before going through some ritual incantations. Swaying backwards and forwards, his necklace with its lizard's tail, dead snake, primate skull, bones, vegetables, and shark's teeth banging rhythmically on his bare chest, he would then scatter the contents of a leather bag on the reed mat between him and his patient.

The medicine man would then proceed to explain the positions of the pieces, pointing to the marble, a dice, a shark's tooth, some animal's egg or a monkey's skull in the process, and make his diagnosis. There would be the offer of medicine, or simply some advice. Then the patient would leave, placing some money in the hollowed tree-stump at the entrance of the kraal.

Neal watched with interest. Eventually it was his turn, and he stumbled awkwardly forward.

'I wonder if you can help me?' he began.

The witch doctor's eyes narrowed. He nodded slightly.

'I have a pregnant maid who is ill, and our white medicine seems to be inactive . . .'

Nongoma pursed his lips. 'What do you think I have to do with that?' he demanded aggressively.

'Sorry, I don't mean to imply you are responsible. I just thought that perhaps we could try some of yours?'

The witch doctor frowned. There was a long pause while he studied Neal, probing for a crack in the façade, dissecting him, looking for the twitch of a muscle.

Total silence descended on the gathering, squeezing the adrenalin into Neal's circulation, making his head pound. He wanted to look away, but the witch doctor's gaze was transfixing.

'What is wrong with your maid?' the witch doctor asked finally.

'She complains of an awful tummy ache, often rolling around on the floor in agony, screaming that the tokolosh has possessed her.'

As he talked, so Neal could see the witch doctor's tensed shoulders drop. But the eyes did not warm.

'We have given her antacids but it has done her no good,' he continued, gaining confidence. 'She keeps calling out for some mushroom—at least, that's what I think she was saying. She seems quite confused.'

Neal paused, studying the man in front of him. All he saw was his nose flare as the witch doctor took a deep breath.

'So I have come to you,' he continued. 'Our medicine seems inactive against her illness. I thought perhaps you have this mushroom, that is if you think it would help.'

'Hmm,' Nongoma replied. 'And you expect me to believe that a white man suddenly sees the virtues of black medicine?'

Neal stiffened. His vulnerable position in the black township suddenly hit home. He had to dig himself out.

'I keep an open mind,' he stammered. 'If a drug works, I use it. And if a patient believes a drug works, that in itself is sometimes enough . . .'

'Hmm.' Nongoma continued staring, suspicion still not

leaving his face. Then he turned towards his bag of dice. He had made up his mind. 'Let us see.'

The medicine man cast the diagnostic dice. With the occasional nod to himself, he interpreted the configuration in silence. Then, ignoring Neal, he twisted round and called to his assistant. Something was whispered in Zulu, whereupon the assistant disappeared inside the kraal, soon to return with a clump of mushrooms.

'Mash these.' Nongoma handed the plants to Neal. 'And give them to your maid. The tokolosh will not resist.'

The witch doctor nodded in dismissal, and Neal was in no mood to disobey.

'Thank you very much indeed.'

The medicine man did not react. He simply stared straight ahead.

Neal walked stiffly across to the tree-stump, unnerved by the consultation. He left a five-rand note. He hoped it had been worth it.

Nongoma excused himself from the market place and returned to the kraal.

From old man Zondi's description, he recognized the doctor. He had seen him at the hospital too, and he was sure it was him. He would have to be stopped, and stopped fast.

However, patients could not be deserted. And there was also an alibi to think about.

'Johannes?' he addressed his assistant.

'Yes, boss.'

'Did you see that white man?'

'Yes, boss.'

'You know what to do?'

'I think so.'

'Remember, boy, make it look like an accident.'

'Yes, boss.'

'But most of all, do a good job. Now go!'

'Yes, boss.'

Then the assistant was gone.

*

While Neal guided his old car away from the township, his thoughts stayed back at the market place. The conviction that the medicine man knew a lot more would not go away.

'That's it!' he remembered. 'Zondi said that the medicine man had told him that other women had become psychotic. How the hell does he know about the post-partum cases? Unless he is responsible . . .'

But that line of reasoning didn't seem to make sense.

'If he's driving women mad by giving them this offending medicine, how come he's prepared to give a sample to me?'

Before Neal could reconcile these recalcitrant facts, the Fiat shuddered sideways with a shattering crash.

'What the hell!' he shouted, fighting to control the car.

It skidded on the loose gravel, sliding briefly off the road on to the embankment and coming dangerously close to the edge of the cliffs. Neal's heart accelerated violently as he caught a glimpse of the rocks below. The sudden dilation of his blood vessels made him momentarily dizzy. He had to shake his head to clear it.

It was then that he saw it. A big green limousine, and it was pulling alongside.

'Jesus!' he shouted, realizing what was happening. 'He's trying to drive me off the road!'

Neal braked furiously, but it was a mistake. The gravel road was covered in patches by soft sand blown up from the sea, patches on which it was fatal to brake.

The Fiat suddenly seemed to float on air, beginning a spin. Reflexly, Neal released his foot. The car slammed into the side of the limousine, suddenly righting itself, and knocking the other vehicle away. For once Neal thanked the car for being there.

He focused his concentration on the road ahead, and on the green limousine in his peripheral vision. There were about three miles of tortuous road along the edge of the cliffs still to go.

Would he make it? He drove his foot down on the accelerator.

The large green car slammed into the small Fiat again, bashing it off the road once more. Being prepared for it hardly made any difference, and Neal had to fight desperately once again to control the car, to keep it from spinning, to direct it away from the cliff's edge.

When he came to steer the car back on to the road, Neal found that the large car had been faster. It now occupied the left-hand lane blocking his retreat from the vertiginous edge.

The Fiat bumped and lurched along the grassy edge, jolting Neal violently in his seat, softening him up for the final blow. Options were few and far between. Braking would have been insane, and the thick grass on the verge made overtaking impossible. The only easy way was over the edge.

Instinctively Neal swung the Fiat into the side of the limousine, hoping to catch the driver unawares. The two cars collided with a deafening crash, banging apart immediately. The larger car swung away, briefly leaving the lane open. Neal was ready and accelerated the Fiat off the bumpy embankment back on to the road.

Suddenly over the rise came a truck carrying sugar cane. Neal bit his lip, his heart in his mouth. He held the Fiat in its lane, hoping the truck-driver would do the same. Then the green limousine would have only one choice. One sensible choice.

The truck thundered by and disappeared into the dust. Neal prayed the dust trail would last the two or so remaining miles. The driver of the limousine would be a fool to try to locate and ram him in that.

But the dust settled too quickly. And out of it emerged the green limousine. It was time for something else.

The dirt road flirted dangerously with the edge of the cliff for the next half a mile. Then it turned away from the sea and down the rolling hills. If it was going to happen, it was going to be in the next few moments.

Neal slowed the car, bracing himself for the next blow, gripping the wheel with a fierce determination. The limou-

sine slammed into the Fiat again, knocking the lighter car
sideways on to the embankment.

Neal battled to control the wheel, pulling the car away
from the edge. He was quicker this time, and the Fiat
slithered back on to the dirt road once more.

There was another 400 yards to go. Neal slowed the car
further and waited. He saw the limousine move out. This was
the moment. He slammed his foot down on the accelerator.

The Fiat jerked forwards just as the limousine swerved
violently inwards. With inches to spare, the Fiat dashed
ahead of the limousine. The larger car encountered only a
trail of dust where Neal's car should have been, bounced
on to the embankment and plunged over the cliff.

'Whew!' Neal let out a huge sigh. 'That was close.'

Relief brought with it that retrospective terror that emergency makes impossible to experience. For a second time in
a week he had nearly wound up on the forensic slab, and
he didn't like it. His life was becoming too cheap.

Maybe I should stop investigating, he suggested to himself.

In another half an hour he was in the hospital car park. An
inspection of the damage revealed ugly dents and scratches
down the one side of the car. Then the Chemical Pathology
Laboratory called.

The hospital was dead. No flow of busy corpuscles down
its long arteries. It was cleaning-up time, and a metal bucket
clanged and sloshed its liquid contents on to the floor in the
entrance hall. Only the cleaners disturbed the once busy
corridors.

At the end of the hall he took the lift down to the
laboratory, feeling once again a return of excitement. Was
he right about the LSD?

He found McKenzie sitting with his bearded chin in his
hands staring at the computer read-out. He only noticed
Neal's presence when he walked up to the bench. He looked
dreadful. A night's sleep did not seem to have helped: his
shoulders sagged with exhaustion, there were black rings
under his eyes, and his face was deathly pale.

'What's up?' Neal asked.

'We were right about the LSD. It's got a different bloody structure, all right. And we were right about it taking longer to be excreted from the system.' McKenzie paused. 'But you can forget about any innocent explanations.'

Neal held his breath.

'The women are not mistakenly eating some natural source of LSD. The sinister fact is that somebody has been injecting them full of LSD. The blood samples you gave me contained LSD decanoate.'

He paused, letting this sink in. When he saw Neal's dazed expression, he decided to elaborate.

'You forgotten what decanoate esters are?'

He shook his head in mock sarcasm.

'It's like the depot medication that you give in the treatment of schizophrenics—fluphenazine decanoate, and fluphenthixol decanoate. As you know, these forms of medication are specially engineered to sit in the muscle tissue so that they constantly dribble their therapeutic effect into the blood over weeks, even months, to keep the patients well.'

He paused again.

'Except that what we have here doesn't cure madness. LSD decanoate does just the opposite. It sits in the muscle and leaks pure madness into the veins.'

CHAPTER 21

'Jee-sus!'

Neal was staggered. Long-acting preparations of anti-psychotic drugs had been available for the treatment of schizophrenia for a number of years, and they enabled a patient's psychosis to be controlled for weeks at a time. The drug was injected intramuscularly and acted as a depot, maintaining a therapeutic level of the drug over long periods.

Now it looked as if someone was using the same method to keep people permanently psychotic.

He slumped on to a free laboratory stool. The satisfaction of finding they had been right was quickly dissipated by the weight of the discovery.

'Is there any way that this form might occur naturally?' he asked half-heartedly.

'No way. LSD decanoate can't be absorbed from the gut—it would be destroyed by gastric acid. So even if there is a naturally occurring form, it would have to be injected for it to have a sustained effect.'

McKenzie paused to let his words sink in. 'But once you accept that these women have to be injected, you have to assume foul play. The question is how? And who?'

Neal, temporarily stunned by having his suspicions justified, found his voice. 'Jill wondered whether Professor Brandsma was driving the women mad. We all know his politics, and that his mental state, as exemplified by his outburst in the Case Presentation last Thursday, is somewhat dodgy . . .'

McKenzie raised an eyebrow.

'I know "dodgy" doesn't appear in the Ninth International Classification of Diseases, but you know what I mean. The man's is a monomaniac. He would do anything to depopulate the southern continent of blacks.'

Neal paused to emphasize his point.

'So he has to be our number one suspect. He has the motive. We all know he would like to stop blacks reproducing, and he could achieve this by driving the women mad and having them stuck away in some remote asylum. He has the means, too. It would be easy enough for anyone with medical training to acquire the ability to synthesize LSD decanoate. And he has the opportunity. These women pass through his hands. In fact, the only doctor consistently linked with the women is Brandsma. He has to be the one who is doing it.

'In fact, I've already approached him, just to sound him out. I fed him some story that I was interested in post-partum psychosis, and wanted to do some research. He didn't like it one bit, though he tried hard not to show it. He said he was doing some work in the same area himself, and wanted no interference from me. He was willing to let me look at his other cases, but wanted the whole thing kept secret, saying he didn't want anyone else making any discoveries before him. He even wanted me to keep Jill Bates, his registrar, away—'

'Let's forget whodunit,' McKenzie interrupted. 'We can't say at this point who is behind it. But what we do know is that patients passing through Brandsma's firm end up getting depot preparations of LSD. What we have to do is to figure out how it's being done. If we can do that, we'll have our man.'

'OK.' Neal took up the thread. 'Let's think of what drugs the obstetric cases might be given?'

'Right. Most of the patients will be given some form of analgæsia during labour, intramuscular pethidine, for example. Someone could be switching the pethidine for depot LSD . . .'

'Brilliant! I could collect some samples in a minute, Mark, if you're up to it. We can test them for LSD.'

'I've revived. Sure.'

Neal scratched his head. 'Jeepers! My obstetrics is a bit rusty. How else might the LSD be given?'

'There is the IM ergometrine,' McKenzie continued. 'I went through Brandsma's firm as a house officer, and he gives his patients IM ergometrine before the delivery of the placenta. He reckons it gives them a more sustained uterine contraction than intravenous ergot. So there's another ampoule we will have to check out. I can't think of any other intramuscular drug.'

There was a pause while both men rehearsed a hypothetical labour.

'OK. Here's what we will do,' Neal said finally. 'I'll go and get some ampoules of IM pethidine and IM ergometrine from Brandsma's labour wards. You can get the mass spectrometer ready.'

Then he remembered something.

'Maybe we shouldn't assume that LSD is given in the hospital. Maybe the witch doctor is giving the drug after all?' he proposed, the terrifying ride back to the hospital uppermost in his mind.

'I've never heard of witch doctors giving injections,' McKenzie countered.

Neal reluctantly agreed. He had just remembered that Selina had taken hers by mouth.

'I'm off, then.'

Neal left the laboratory lost in thought. His footsteps echoed down the long corridors, making him feel even more detached and unreal. The idea of someone driving people mad with depot LSD was incredible and he was having difficulty accepting it.

What puzzled him was the rationality of the perpetrator. If he was doing it to reduce the numbers of blacks in South Africa, surely there were more effective means, like tying off the women's tubes? Driving them mad did not make much sense.

He was soon at the lift and on his way to the fifteenth floor. He wondered if he had any adrenalin left, it had been such a traumatic day. But as he walked out of the lift, he had his answer. He could feel his pulse quicken, his hands moisten.

Suites 05 and 06 were at the end of the noisy corridor. Unlike the rest of the hospital, the labour ward was busy as usual—babies did not have any respect for a doctor's weekend. There was the usual screaming and wailing of women in labour, harmonizing badly with the bellowed instructions from the midwives.

'Doctor! Can we help?' The question was more like a threat.

Neal turned to see a large black midwife coming towards him. He had forgotten that in the labour ward, the midwife was queen.

He tried not to let his voice betray his anxiety. 'Um . . . Sister, I am doing some research into stress in labour—it has departmental approval, don't worry, and I won't be interfering with you or your staff—' he lied, hoping that the midwife would accept the explanation.

'See that you don't, young man. See that you don't!'

With that, the midwife turned on her heel and walked down to the opposite end of the corridor. Neal gave a mental sigh of relief, and headed for 05.

It was going to be difficult to get into the medicine cabinet unless a patient was in second stage. Then it was usually left open in case of emergencies. He stuck his head round 05. There was a large lady on the trolley, but the cardiotocograph was still on, and he knew enough to remember that this meant she was still in the first stage of labour.

He peeped into 06 and the first thing he saw was the short figure of Isaacs. He wrenched himself back.

What the hell is he doing here? he wondered. He did not like the way the administrator was popping up in all the wrong places.

He took another brief look into the delivery suite. The patient was in lithotomy and it was all hands on deck. This was the right moment, but he needed a disguise.

Just then a male student walked out of the adjacent room. In a flash Neal had introduced himself, explaining that he was studying the psychological effects of labour but didn't want to be noticed. That was why he wanted to borrow the student's name badge. Just for half an hour.

Neal left the perplexed student to revive himself in the student canteen and collected a gown and mask at the entrance to 06 to complete his disguise. It was standard gear for the second stage, but Neal was not wearing it for the newborn's benefit. Then he slipped quietly into the delivery room.

The woman in lithotomy was obviously in considerable pain. Her face was contorted into an ugly mask and she was moaning and writhing on the trolley. At her side was a midwife holding her hand, rubbing her brow in an attempt to ease the distress, giving soothing words of comfort. But to no avail.

There was a registrar standing between her stirruped legs, cutting a large episiotomy. Neal could just make out the dark head of the baby in the birth canal, and presumed the second stage had arrested. Another midwife was fussing around the registrar, trying to satisfy his wishes by holding as many instruments as she could manage.

'Forceps!' the registrar barked.

Neal ignored the action and looked around for the medicine cabinet. It was on the far side of the bed, and when he located it, he moved quietly behind the midwife and registrar, keeping an eye on Isaacs.

The administrator didn't react. If he had seen Neal, he gave no sign of it. He seemed lost in his thoughts, staring vacantly ahead. Anyway, there was nothing unusual in students coming in to see how it was done.

Neal waited till the forceps had been applied before he eased the cabinet door open. It gave out an awful creak, and the midwife turned at the sound. Neal froze.

'What the hell do you think you're doing?'

'Sister . . .' Neal stammered, seeing Isaacs turn his head in their direction, 'I thought I would hand you the ergometrine for—'

'Sister!' the registrar bellowed. 'Pay bloody attention, will you! We have a strangulating cord here.'

The sister gave Neal another glare, as if to say he would get his talking-to later, and turned to clamp the cord twisted around the child's neck.

Neal took his opportunity. The door was open, and he scanned the ampoules for ergometrine and pethidine. An excuse for overtly searching the cabinet had been given, and he no longer tried to conceal his actions.

It took him a while to spot the correct drawer, and when he did he hurriedly pulled it open to expose rows of glass ampoules. With cold wet hands, he grabbed a clump of them, and keeping his back to Isaacs, stuffed them into his pocket. Then he waited with a single ergometrine ampoule for the cord to be cut.

When two clamps had been fixed on the cord, the midwife

produced a pair of surgical scissors and cut it. With that
the single umbilical artery sprayed the green coats of the
attendants with splodges of blood. Then the registrar pulled
the child's head down, hooking his finger under the armpit
and giving the shoulder a pull. It slipped under the symphy-
sis pubis, and as it emerged, the sister turned her angry face
to Neal once more.

He was ready, and thrust the ampoule in her direction.
There was no time for a lecture, and she had to content
herself with a brusque grab.

Neal did not wait around for his lecture. As the sister was
swabbing the patient's buttock, he made a move for the
door.

'Hey, you!' It was Isaacs.

For an instant, Neal wondered if he should stop. He
would be found with addictive drugs in his pocket—
that wouldn't have looked good, so he kept going, ducking out of the delivery room and running down the
corridor.

'Stop this instant!'

A rapid staccato of footsteps started down the corridor
after him, and soon he could hear panting and wheezing.
Thankfully, Neal was in better shape.

He swept past the lifts and headed for the stairs. There
was no point getting caught waiting for the lift to stagger
up from the basement. As he bounded down, taking two
steps at a time, he saw Isaacs stop at the lift.

Neal kept to the stairs while checking the lift on each floor
for Isaacs's progress. The lights eventually reached fifteen,
and then began to descend slowly. He watched the descent
of the lift to the ground floor—Isaacs obviously assumed
that he would try to leave the building. It was time to get
rid of his disguise; time to take the lift at the other end of
the building to the basement.

When he arrived back at the laboratory, still out of breath,
McKenzie had everything prepared.

'Any joy?'

'Yessir.'

'Good. I think what I'll do is to programme the mass spectrometer with the fingerprint of LSD decanoate, and see whether we get a match,' McKenzie explained.

'Sounds reasonable to me. We already know the chemical formula of the sample,' Neal agreed, setting down his precious ampoules on the bench.

McKenzie shoved a koki pen in his direction. 'Label them, will you? Numerically.'

Neal began labelling, and McKenzie produced a pipette from the bench drawer and snapped open the first ampoule, sucking up half a millilitre which he then decanted into a labelled test-tube. He then carefully repeated the procedure till he had sampled all the 13 ampoules Neal had managed to remove from the ward.

He then placed the first test-tube into the hole in the mass spectrometer marked SAMPLE, and typed in 'Sample added. Please fingerprint.'

'Each chemical absorbs certain colours from natural light to provide a unique pattern which can be used to identify it,' McKenzie explained.

There was a great whirring in the machine, and the monitor produced a graph with spectral absorption bands. McKenzie typed in the command 'Match with LSD decanoate'.

They held their breath.

The spectral lines of LSD decanoate flashed on to the graph in a different colour. The lines didn't coincide with the sample's, and the monitor flashed agreement: NO MATCH. McKenzie asked the mass spectrometer to match with pethidine, and they received a perfect match.

'The first one is innocent, unfortunately,' McKenzie concluded.

He turned and took the next test-tube and fed it into the mass spectrometer. He repeated the procedure, and asked the spectrometer if the sample was LSD decanoate. They waited again with bated breath, and again the monitor flashed NO MATCH.

'Shit!' Neal cursed.

'Hold on,' McKenzie cautioned. 'If at first you don't succeed . . .'

They continued to analyse the ampoules with little success. Neal began to wonder if they had left something out. There were other theories that hadn't been eliminated. Perhaps the women received an intramuscular injection from a private supply of the drug. Perhaps they received the injection outside the hospital grounds. Perhaps it was the witch doctor after all.

McKenzie fed in sample 11. The spectrometer whirred, and the mesmerizing words POSITIVE MATCH began to pulse on the screen, reflecting off two appalled faces.

An ampoule of ergometrine contained depot LSD.

CHAPTER 22

At the Umzimkulu Rehabilitation Unit, Jill decided it was time to venture out. It required some nerve, but she had given herself a pep talk and felt a little better.

When she tried to stand she found her legs were jelly-like, and she had to steady herself on the bed to prevent herself toppling over. Her feet had gone to sleep. Letting herself slip to the floor, she began massaging her numb legs back to life, as she forced herself to think of a plan.

She knew that she would have to stay within the confines of the building until the dogs were chained, and this probably meant till morning. She had at least that long to find out what was going on in the Umzimkulu Rehabilitation Unit.

She tried her legs again. They worked. Cautiously she made her way to the entrance of the ward. At the door she paused and listened. There was only the sighing respiration of patients asleep.

What were they doing with the patient? Perhaps she had developed acute appendicitis and they were transferring her to a waiting ambulance. But then why would they have bleeped a doctor? It didn't seem to make much sense, unless they were going to operate in the building.

Unless they have planned a tubal ligation for this evening, she reminded herself ominously. The ease with which that theory seemed to explain the men's actions that evening made her feel uncomfortable. She ventured out into the dark and deserted corridor.

She stuck close to the wall, using the pillars again for cover. The light from the central wing illuminated the hallway, casting a ghostly light on the bald head of the bust guarding the entrance to the building.

'Some pompous benefactor, no doubt,' Jill muttered.

Before entering the central wing, she glanced briefly around the corner. The corridor seemed awfully long, the harsh light unwelcoming. Jill clenched her teeth, and moved stealthily down the right-hand wall.

She reached the end of the corridor without incident. It ended in a small hallway on which five doors opened, making her feel like Alice in Wonderland. She hoped she would make the right choice. She eased up to the first, and listened.

There was nothing. She was about to try the second, when her ears picked up the sound of a car on gravel.

'Oh God! The doctor's arriving!' she whispered.

For a moment she panicked, standing fixed to the spot. She knew it was time that she disappeared from view, but there were not many choices. She moved back to the first door and tried the handle. It was open.

She found herself in an illuminated operating theatre. In the centre was the patient strapped to the trolley and surrounded by trays of surgical instruments. She ducked inside.

Her heart began pounding in her head, making it difficult to think. She began to feel light-headed, and a curious distance seemed to yawn up between her and the world. She shook her head as if to rid herself of the anxiety. Her thoughts had dried up when she needed them most. Wrenching her gaze from the patient in the centre, she looked around the theatre. It was almost completely bare, devoid of cover.

A door slammed in the hallway, followed by footsteps approaching. Time had run out. She had to act.

The footsteps stopped, and the muffled sound of a conversation drifted through the door. Jill hardly registered. Her eyes were darting around the room again, seeking any sign of retreat.

'Was that the Doc arriving?' one voice said.

'Ja. Have you got everything ready?'

'Sweet, my man. Just sweet.'

'Is the woman ready?'

'Hey, man, everything is cool. Relax.'

Jill knew she did not have much longer. Her eyes fixed once more on the patient on the trolley. The woman was lying on green drapes which were hanging over the edge like curtains.

Like curtains! Jill could have kicked herself.

It was a slim chance, but one she would have to take. She darted into the centre of the room and pulled aside one of the drapes. To her relief, there was a base to the trolley about a foot off the ground, holding the patient's crumpled nightdress, her slippers, and a small cup containing her false teeth. Jill climbed on, pushing the clothes aside, pulling the drapes back, and huddled herself into a ball. It wasn't much, but it would have to do.

The door banged open and the two nurses sauntered into the operating theatre, talking as they walked.

'Have you been monitoring her?'

'Ja. A little. There isn't much time left, I know that. No sign of distress, either.'

'I see you haven't used the monitor. Won't the Doc be cheesed off?'

'Stay cool, man, things are under control. The Doc doesn't believe in high tech for its own sake.'

They walked up to the patient who had begun moaning. The moaning began to increase in decibels and the trolley vibrated as the woman tossed with distress. Jill had to hold on to the legs to prevent herself from being shaken out.

'The pethidine seems to be wearing off. I reckon we let her wail.'

'Sure.'

Wailing and screaming was exactly what the woman was doing, and the noise in the tiled room was deafening, so deafening that Jill did not hear the theatre door slam and the 'Doc' walk in. Only when he was standing one foot away did Jill suddenly spot the surgically clad legs, an she jumped involuntarily. She watched as he examined the patient, steadying herself as the trolley rocked in the process.

It was clear that this was a surgical emergency. The woman was obviously in pain, and she presumed that was why the 'Doc' had been called. This was no elective tubal ligation.

The wailing subsided, and a new voice muffled by a surgical mask could be heard.

'It should be about an hour. Give me a buzz, will you.'

'Right.'

The man in surgical apparel turned and walked towards the door, his rubber boots squeaking on the floor and giving Jill runs of goose bumps. As the theatre door slammed, so the patient on the bed began moaning again, and the trolley shook once more with her writhings. The moaning soon became a deafening scream, and Jill covered her ears to dull the sound.

Why are they waiting? she asked herself; why is the pain coming in waves? Then she nearly bumped her head on the roof of the trolley as the truth sank in. *Of course! She is in labour!*

What this meant she had no idea. The woman might have been admitted pregnant, or she might have become pregnant in the asylum. The second alternative sounded rather ominous. What was going on?

While Jill crouched under the trolley puzzling over these strange events, the woman on the trolley endured waves of pain, periodically almost bursting Jill's eardrums. They were giving her no analgæsia, presumably for the baby's sake.

The next hour passed more rapidly than Jill would have thought possible in such an uncomfortable position. She assumed it was an hour when the nurses stopped chatting and one of them came round to the foot of the trolley to do a vaginal examination.

'She's ready to pop. Go buzz the Doc, will you?'

The other nurse tramped across the theatre floor and disappeared out of sight. In a few moments the door swung open again and the 'Doc' led the way into the room. Jill desperately wanted to discover the identity of the man, but could not risk exposing herself. She had to content herself with looking at his surgically clad legs.

'Fully dilated, you were saying?' It was the muffled voice of the 'Doc'.

The voice was strangely familiar. But then every voice sounded the same behind a surgical mask. He was doing another vaginal examination, and the trolley shook with his probing.

'Stick up the stirrups, will you? I want her in lithotomy,' the 'Doc' commanded.

The rest of the conversation was lost in another crescendo of screams from the patient. The three men busied themselves around the trolley, bumping and jostling it and keeping Jill on her toes. Occasionally, above the screams, Jill could hear instructions to the mother: '*Dunza, Mama, Dunza!*' Then screams began to mutate into throaty grunts, and Jill guessed the baby was crowning.

'Scissors!'

There followed the unpleasant sound of taut flesh being sliced apart. The next thing Jill saw was a flood of liquor and blood gushing over the end of the trolley, and with that the baby was tugged into the world.

Now there was another cry in the theatre, an impotent but healthy protest from the new arrival. From the way the men were clapping and cheering, the birth had gone well. They seemed very pleased with themselves.

'Looks perfect! Wonderful! Wrap him up. We don't want to disappoint the parents.'

Jill missed what was said next. She watched the blood drip from the open episiotomy scar, and wondered at a doctor who did not want to disappoint the mother with a sick infant, but who was prepared to let her bleed. It didn't make sense.

'Time for a celebration, I think. Its number one hundred.'

'Congratulations, boss!'

'No, no. It's thanks to you guys as well. What do you say to a drink in my office?'

The nurses accepted.

'Just plug the episiotomy, will you? We don't want a body to dispose of,' the 'Doc' ordered.

Jill watched with relief as the three men walked out of the theatre, talking and clapping one another on the back as they went. Then the theatre was returned to relative quiet. Only the feeble moans of the mother could be heard.

It was time to get out of there. Jill guessed the men were in one of the other three rooms leading off the hall and reckoned she probably had five minutes, five very short minutes to get down the central wing to the safety of the wards. She hoped her feet would work this time.

She pulled the drape to one side, helping her cramped leg on to the theatre floor with her hand. She tried it, and it held. Then, using her hand to pull her other leg out, she stood up.

Swaying initially, she steadied herself on the trolley. With some effort and considerable pain, she straightened her back, and gazed at the obese black woman on the trolley. The woman was exhausted and pale. Judging from the pool of blood on the floor, she had lost at least half a litre. If they left her any longer, she would soon die of shock.

If I stay around, I'm not going to survive much longer either! Jill reminded herself.

As she moved towards the door, she noticed the plastic cot next to the bed, and could not resist a quick look at the baby.

She was not ready for what she saw. No theory she had been conjuring with could have prepared her. She was not even sure whether she should trust her senses.

She looked again at the cot, shaking her head in disbelief. The image was the same. It was a child all right. And it was a healthy child. But it was not black, or coloured.

It was as Caucasian a baby as Jill had ever seen.

CHAPTER 23

Jill had to jam the thoughts flooding into her consciousness. This was not the time for the luxury of speculation—there was her own skin to think about. The three men were still celebrating, judging from the muffled laughter penetrating into the theatre, but it wouldn't last all night.

Tearing her feet from their rivets, she darted across the theatre, pausing briefly at the door only to listen. More muffled laughter. She eased the theatre door open, peering around it to survey the hallway. It was clear.

Jill knew there was no time for half-measures, and in her bare feet she tore down the corridor towards the ward. She could feel her back prickle in anticipation, she could almost hear the pursuing footsteps. But no door opened, no 'Hey, you!' halted her progress.

The corner seemed to take an interminably long time to arrive, remaining in the distance like a haven in a nightmare. Even her running seemed to be in slow motion. No matter how hard she tried, she could not speed it up.

Then all at once she was at the corner, and she reached out to reassure herself. It was real. She turned right, but jolted herself to a halt.

'They will be returning the mother to her bed. I'd better go to the other ward,' she reasoned.

She fled quietly down the corridor to the ward that had sheltered her before. It was peaceful and quiet, and she was not about to recreate Bedlam. Jill found her old bed, hoping it would bring her luck, and disappeared beneath it.

She let out a long sigh. She had made it. In about five minutes, her pulse had slowed, her rebound shakiness had gone. She had time to think.

'What in heaven's name is going on?' she whispered aloud, almost forgetting where she was. 'Am I going mad, or is it the world that is cracking up?'

She closed her eyes, but there was no respite. All she could see was the perfectly formed newborn, perfect except that he had been the wrong colour.

If she wasn't going mad and it had been a white child in the cot, she had tumbled on to something awful. How could a black mother give birth to a wholly Caucasian child? It couldn't happen naturally.

It was possible the child was an albino. But when she conjured the image of him in her mind's eye, she knew that this was not on. The hair had been brown—there was no defective melanin synthesis there.

But if it couldn't happen naturally, what dreadful experiment was being carried out? She had no idea. The only thing she knew was that she couldn't let herself be discovered.

Then, suddenly, she knew. The women were being kidnapped and used as surrogate mothers. Used as surrogate mothers to increase the birth rate of the Afrikaners. She had made a colossal mistake. Brandsma was not driving the women insane to prevent them reproducing. Quite the opposite. They were being held there to reproduce, but not to reproduce themselves. They were being held to reproduce the Afrikaner race. They were part of a plan for the rebirth of the Afrikaner in South Africa!

Jill paused and wondered at her imagination.

It was then that she remembered what had prompted her to come to the Umzimkulu Rehabilitation Unit. It had been the recorded telephone message. Now she could understand it. The woman was not a black being directed to the asylum for some tubal ligation. The woman was a white being told where to collect yet another Afrikaner baby.

Jill took a deep breath. She had to get out of there. She had to get help. She had to last the night.

All of a sudden she realized how exhausted she was. There was little point in trying to keep watch—her eyelids were far too heavy.

She must have drifted off to sleep, for she gradually became aware that someone was tugging her by the shoulder and shaking her awake. Panic struck at her chest, and she tried to turn to see what was holding her fast, expecting to see the ugly face of the nursing officer leering at her. But she couldn't see anyone.

She continued to struggle, kicking frantically in all directions, out of control. She was held by the scruff of her neck in a vice, and any effort was useless. She wanted to scream, but her voice had deserted her.

She struggled again, and surfaced fully from her sleep, drenched and unsettled. The bedsprings had tangled in her jumper and were tugging her as she rolled over.

She stopped struggling, composed herself, and listened. The ward was stirring to an orchestra of birds. It was daytime, and judging from the angle of the sun streaming into the ward, it was just after sunrise.

Jill collected her scattered and anxious thoughts as she twisted round to disentangle herself. She remembered all too vividly the events of the previous night, reminding herself of her vulnerable position. And there were the dogs to think about.

She wondered how she could negotiate them. Perhaps she could use the patients again. By coaxing a patient outside, it wouldn't be long before she learned whether the dogs were still out. South African dogs had a special dislike for blacks.

But the idea was dismissed at once. She couldn't use a patient as bait.

There was a possibility she could spot the dogs wandering around the garden, or better still, chained up. She eased herself out from her hiding-place and peered over the sea of beds.

There was no enemy in sight. Just waves of restless patients surfacing from troubled sleep. She crawled on all fours to the window at the end of the ward and scanned the outside world.

The grounds surrounding the home were barren, dry grass burnt by the African sun, punctuated by the occasional thorn tree. Few shady places that could shelter dogs. No kennels. And no dogs. Jill was just about to try the other ward when she heard a door slam somewhere down the corridor. She dived out of sight.

Footsteps were coming down the corridor, and voices drifted into the ward. The nurses were doing an early round. Then the door to the ward was flung open and the two nurses entered the ward.

'What time did you say they were coming?'

'Hang loose, man. Doc said they would be here in an hour. Apparently they couldn't wait.'

'Is everything ready?'

'Ja, man. Don't hassle.'

The two nurses set about getting the patients up and herding them out of the ward.

Probably breakfast-time, Jill surmised. The Afrikaner fœtuses need to be fed.

When things were quiet again, she decided it was time to make a break for it. She guessed the new parents were about to arrive, eager to see the latest Afrikaner baby. If everything was ready, as the nurses had intimated, that had to mean that the bull-mastiffs were chained up. There was no point in having the prospective parents chewed alive.

Jill poked her head out of the ward. There was nobody in sight. Still barefoot, she tiptoed down the corridor towards the marble statue guarding the hallway, towards the entrance, towards freedom.

The front door was heavy oak, and she had to lean back to creak it slowly open. Squinting in the harsh sunlight, she surveyed the scene. It was clear.

She was just about to make a dash for it when she saw him. A thickset man clad in a nurse's uniform heading towards the gate, presumably to unlock it. And then he would turn around . . .

Feeling suddenly naked, Jill cast about for somewhere to hide. The first thing that caught her eye also made up her mind. It was a dusty yellow delivery van. What it delivered, Jill had no idea. But it might deliver her her freedom.

She leapt down the stairs, dashed across the stony driveway, and pressed herself behind the back of the van in time to see the nurse turn back. The back door was not locked. Jill eased it open and slipped inside.

There were a few crates marked FRAGILE stacked inside, and little else. Closing the door behind her, Jill crawled into a corner and pulled two crates around as cover. There was little time to worry if the crates were coming or going. Her last card had been played.

With blood pounding in her ears, making it difficult to hear, Jill was able to follow the nurse coming back to the asylum, have a brief conversation at the entrance, and then return to the van. Mercifully, he didn't bother looking at his goods. The driver's door opened, and clattered shut, jolting the inside of the van. Then they were off.

It was not a comfortable way to travel—the van's suspension was about as faded as its colour, but Jill was not about to complain. The more distance between her and the Umzimkulu Rehabilitation Unit, the better.

She tried to occupy her mind by calculating where they were going, straining to keep her sense of direction, timing the journey and estimating their speed. A half-hour later, when the van braked and shuddered to a stop, Jill reckoned they were probably somewhere in Durban. With luck.

She braced herself. Half an hour had been enough to decide on a course of action. If the back door was opened, the nurse was going to be greeted by a crate full in the face. Then she would have to make a run for it.

The driver's door opened. There were footsteps on the road. The nurse was walking away. The unexpected threw her. Having made a plan, she found it more comfortable than the unforeseen. Then the footsteps faded. There was silence, and no traffic could be heard. Was this Durban? Where were they? Did the nurse know she was there?

Panic finally took over. Jill pushed the crate aside, twisted the inside latch and blasted her eyes with billions of energetic rays of sunlight. There were no houses. No cars. No pavements. She was in the bush.

Suspended half-way out of the van, Jill tried to think. She could hide in the long grass. That seemed safe, but it might take her hours, days even, to get home. Or she could remain in the van, hoping the next stop would be Durban. That too was risky.

All her deliberation was in vain.

'*Wat maak jy daar?*' the nurse shouted a hundred yards away.

Jill stiffened with fright, bashing her head on the roof of the van, and then toppling out of the van head first. Instinctively, her arms shot forward, and the momentum of her fall jolted into her shoulder-blades, leaving them ringing with pain.

Frantically, she scrambled up, looking around like a hunted animal trying to learn its fate. She had ten seconds. That was all. Fifty yards away the nurse was scrambling up the slope towards her. There was nowhere to run. And she was no athlete. There was no one with whom to shelter. She was on her own.

Jill found herself moving her limbs mechanically in the direction of the driver's seat, feeling suddenly strangely distant, detached from it all. She twisted the door handle and pulled.

Nothing. She pulled again, and this time the door creaked open.

It was then that the nursing officer dived. He caught Jill squarely as she opened the door, crushing her on to the car, and squeezing from her the badly needed air. Jill absorbed the blow, struggling to keep her wits about her. She lashed out violently with her elbow, aiming for his head.

The nurse had not anticipated a struggle. Having made a superhuman effort to catch her, he had relaxed his guard momentarily. Jill's elbow flashed backwards, catching him on the bridge of the nose and snapping it audibly.

He staggered back in surprise, unpinning Jill from the car, and splattering her with a torrent of bright red blood. He had thought it was over, and his staring eyes said as much.

Jill did not hesitate. She wrenched the van door open, swinging it back with all her remaining strength. It swung out, hitting the startled nursing officer in the ribs, and knocking him off balance. Jill flung herself in and locked the door. That might give her the time she needed.

The keys thankfully were still in the ignition, and twisting them violently she waited impatiently as the engine turned over, and then turned over again. Holding her bursting breath, she pleaded with the van to respond.

'Fire, will you. Godammit! Fire!'

The nurse recovered from his surprise and tried the door, his teeth bared in an ugly grin. When the futility sank in, he cast about the ground for something hard, something with which to shatter Jill's fragile and temporary fortress.

Jill did not see any of this. She stared straight ahead, willing the van to start.

'Please, start, for God's sake!'

She did not hear the crash, for as the stone struck the window, shattering its transparent pane into thousands of white fragments that showered the inside of the van, the engine fired and sprang to life.

Jill was only dimly aware of the scattering glass, so focused was her concentration. She was thinking only of escape. Her foot firmly on the accelerator, she gunned the engine before releasing the handbrake. Then she slammed the gear into first.

But the nursing officer was not finished. He thrust his hand through the shattered window and grabbed Jill's throat in a vice. His powerful thumb and index finger jabbed behind the strap muscles of her neck, probing for the carotid arteries. Jill tried to pull the hand off, but the grip was too strong.

She tried to dig her nails into his arm, to wrench it free. But it was hopeless. Dizziness was quick to follow, and her world began to acquire gaping holes and explode with flashing lights. She was fading away.

Her foot slipped off the clutch, and as it did so, the van jerked forwards, pulling the nurse with it. The serrated edge of the window dug into his arm, and his fierce grin loosened. Once more Jill's carotids pulsed reviving oxygen to her thirsting brain and her world came back into focus.

The van was running forwards now, and Jill could see the nurse running alongside, clinging to the door. She grabbed the steering-wheel to gain control of the runaway van, and slammed her foot on to the accelerator. The vehicle jerked forwards and headed up the dirt road.

The nurse lost his footing and fell. But he was not giving up. He doggedly held on to the door and was dragged along by the van, cursing and growling.

Jill could just see his hands in her peripheral vision and prayed that her passenger would not stay very long. She threw the steering-wheel from side to side, desperately trying to throw him off. But he was a tougher customer than she had bargained for.

Then it got worse. He thrust an arm into the car and began to climb in, his snarling face appearing at the window. Looking for a better purchase, he thrust his arm into the car. Then he found a grip.

It was the door handle. In a flash, the handle was elevated and the door flew open, leaving the nurse to swing freely over the rapidly moving road.

There was a sharp curve in the road up ahead. Jill did not hesitate. The van took the corner without stopping, swinging round in an arc, dust billowing behind. The front door swung with centrifugal force through one hundred and eighty degrees, snapping off its safety catch. It slammed the nurse on to the side of the bonnet, shattering his grip and abandoning him to gravity.

The vehicle skidded on the dust round the corner, ditching its unwanted passenger. His limp and almost lifeless body slipped between the door and bonnet and tumbled and scraped its way to a stop on the road. The van sped on, taking only the bloodstains of the nursing officer with it.

Jill let out a huge sigh of relief. She found herself shaking uncontrollably now that she knew it was all over, and she had to slow the van for fear of ploughing into the sugar cane.

She had to find help.

CHAPTER 24

'So what do we do now?'

It was McKenzie who finally broke the silence. The flashing signal of POSITIVE MATCH from the mass spectrometer had thrown them into a trance, and they were having difficulty emerging. It was as if the flashing had induced petit mal seizures.

'Well?' McKenzie repeated his question.

With the spell broken, it was time to think. One thing was clear to Neal. There was a connection between his investigation into the post-partum psychotics and the attempts on his life. He could feel it in his bones.

But was it clear that Brandsma was behind it? If he was trying to stop blacks reproducing, why was he doing it so inefficiently? Secretly tying Fallopian tubes was much more effective. Surely he was not so stupid?

'You know, we have been assuming that Brandsma has been driving black women mad because he wants to stop them reproducing. But it doesn't make sense.' Neal aired his misgivings. 'Why does he just choose obese patients?'

'Well, you told me he was doing research on obesity . . .'

'Yes. But there are other women who go through Brandsma's firm—why doesn't he drive them mad?'

There was a studied pause in the conversation.

'Perhaps the Professor isn't involved,' Neal persisted.

There was another pause.

'I wonder whether we shouldn't confront him with the facts and see how he reacts. If he doesn't suggest going to the police, we will have some reason to suspect him. But if he is not involved, perhaps he can give us an idea of what is going on. What do you think?'

'I think you've got to be crazy,' McKenzie replied. 'If he is involved, he'll finish you off. I'm surprised to hear you talking like this, especially after the attempts on your life.'

'What's your suggestion, then?' Neal asked defensively.

'For me. I'd go to the police right now. Lay it all before them.'

'Ja?' Neal's tone was sarcastic. 'Lay what before them? That some ampoules of ergometrine contain LSD. That's not enough to convict anybody. The police will laugh you out of the station. You have absolutely nothing on the Professor, and such a move would simply drive him into covering up his tracks.'

McKenzie shook his head. 'Well, I'm not about to volunteer for confronting Brandsma. No sirree. Count me out. I have a wife and kid.' McKenzie's words were overdramatic, almost humorous. But he was deadly serious.

Neal straightened his stiff back. He would have to go it alone.

'Listen,' McKenzie tried. 'There is a better strategy. Let's just wait and see, collect more evidence against him. Hell, Neal, if the man has gone to such lengths to secure the supremacy of the Afrikaner in southern Africa, do you think he is going to let the likes of you interfere? Jesus, man, he will probably have the whole of the police force in his pocket as well.'

'Which will make going to the police with more evidence all the more futile too,' Neal replied. 'No, my mind's made up. We can't sit on this.' He stood up. 'Anyway, it's probably better that I go on my own. That way I'll have you as insurance.'

McKenzie nodded. 'I can compile a statement of everything we know about the case and drop it into the post. I'll

address it to Prof. Evans shall I? That way there will be
no point eliminating us.' He paused. 'I know it sounds
melodramatic and all that. But I think we ought to be
cautious. Who knows what sort of stakes ar being played?
And if those attacks on you are connected, they really do
mean business.'

Neal nodded agreement. It made sense. 'Right. I'll see
you. Wish me luck.'

'Break a leg,' McKenzie called.

When Nongoma came, Cedric Zondi was sitting in his
garden thinking about Selina. He hardly recognized the
medicine man, for he was dressed in blue overalls with the
name 'Durban City Council' printed front and back.

'Hau! What is this?' Cedric blurted.

'One for you, my friend. This is the day we check electricity meters.'

'Electricity meters? But why? And where?' Cedric was
confused.

'I have found out where they take the women, old man.
And it is time to pay them a visit.'

'Then we will not be checking electricity meters?' Cedric
was still not following.

'No. You will pretend to check the meters, and I will
snoop around . . .'

'Around where?'

'The Umzimkulu Rehabilitation Unit.'

'God! You're a mess!'

Charge Nurse Hawton dragged himself through the front
door to the Umzimkulu Rehabilitation Unit and almost
tripped in the process. He was not about to disagree.

'What happened, *ou*? You had a fight with the dogs?'

'Na. But we had no sleepwalker last night.'

'What are you talking about? Come on, let me help you.
Betadine and bandages is what you need. And valium.'

Davies put his arm under his colleague's shoulder and
helped him towards the clinic room. Hawton was indeed a

mess. His hands were in shreds, his forearms lacerated and dripping with blood, his nose broken, and his front from his face to his knees had been badly scratched, his clothes torn to expose the peeled inner layers of skin oozing with a yellow clear fluid.

'Now tell me what happened,' Davies repeated as he helped his colleague on to the bed.

'It was a bloody woman—and don't you laugh.'

'Some floozie get the better of you?'

'Bitch! I'll get her.'

Hawton winced with pain as he screwed up his face in anger. Davies let him take his time.

'I think it was her that we heard last night,' Hawton said as Davies helped him off with his shirt. 'And I think that she knows something. The way she fought, it was for her life, man. Like she knew what would happen if she were caught.'

Davies nodded absently. He was concentrating on assessing the wounds.

'We'll have to get after her,' Hawton continued.

'Ja? Just ring up everyone in Durban and ask them if they have just visited the Umzimkulu Rehabilitation Unit?' Davies asked sarcastically.

'No. But I got her car registration number—she left her Mini outside. We can trace her address.'

Neal was soon on the Marine Parade heading for a more affluent part of Durban. The streets were again deserted. It was after one o'clock, and the shops had closed for the weekend. He made good time.

It was not difficult to locate the address: 87 Jan Smuts Avenue, Sea View. Neal soon drew up outside the large mansion looking out over the bay. He turned off the engine and waited. For a while he wondered what he was doing there.

'I'm here because I just don't suspect the man,' he rationalized to himself. 'He'd have to be crazy to be giving his patients LSD. But he's not. Ergo . . .'

Neal was sure that Brandsma was fiercely committed to the supremacy of the Afrikaner, convinced that he was obsessed by it, almost blinded by his passion. But the man was not psychotic.

He pushed the car door open and climbed out. The sign on the gate made him hesitate again. It read: 'Beware the Dog! *Passop die hond!*' It was no welcome.

As soon as Neal had set foot on Brandsma's land, he found himself staring at the bared and snarling teeth of an unfriendly Alsatian. Neal did not move. He hoped that the dog was a racist.

'Stay!' Brandsma bellowed from the veranda.

The Alsatian immediately closed its threatening jaws, wagged its tail, and showed Neal the way round to the veranda. He followed at a safe distance.

Brandsma was sitting on the veranda, drink in hand, reading the *Daily News*. He seemed to be expecting Neal, for he only looked up as Neal stopped in front of him.

'Ja? What have you discovered?'

There was no greeting, no observance of any courtesy. Just the hostile request.

'Sorry to interrupt your afternoon, Professor,' Neal began. 'But I think there is something important you should know.'

'*Ja. Skoot, man! Vind jouself 'n stool.*' Brandsma stuck to his mother tongue, making it more difficult for Neal.

Neal seated himself on the edge of a nearby seat. It was going to be difficult.

'You remember I told you I wanted to study post-partum psychosis?'

'Ja.'

'Well, the fact is, I've already done quite a bit of studying.'

Neal paused, scrutinizing Brandsma's face for any flicker of alarm. But the Professor's face was stonily impassive.

'I've collected eighteen cases, and they all look more like a drug-induced psychosis. But there is something else that is odd. They all came from 05 and 06, the wards where you are running your obesity trial, and end up in a place called the Umzimkulu Rehabilitation Unit.'

Brandsma sat up in his chair. He looked tense.

'We have actually confirmed that these cases of psychosis are drug-induced, in fact by LSD,' Neal continued, patting the Alsatian who was now pawing at his jeans. 'But what is more alarming is that we have discovered the means whereby such women acquire the LSD. We have sampled some of the ampoules allegedly containing ergometrine in 06. Some contain LSD decanoate, a depot form of the hallucinogenic drug.'

Professor Brandsma's eyes widened. 'So *that's* how they do it! God! I've been trying to discover that for months!'

Neal was stunned. 'You . . . you know about this?'

'Of course, man.'

Neal battled to piece things together. 'Why didn't you . . . do something?' he stammered.

'Not enough evidence. And I wanted him myself.'

Brandsma spoke as if his words should be self-explanatory, but Neal just looked blank.

'Listen, Potter. I have known for months that something was going on. Too many of the women in my obesity trial were going mad soon after delivery. Some even killing themselves. Something was going on, and I was convinced it wasn't nice.'

Brandsma stood up and began pacing around.

'I thought it was one of my colleagues trying to discredit me. Everyone knows I dislike the fact that blacks reproduce faster than us whites, and will soon make our supremacy here impossible. Everyone knows I would dearly love to stop them.'

He stopped in his tracks and spun round to face Neal.

'But I am no psychopath. I would not drive women mad. I would not drive them to suicide. When I found out that this was happening in my trial, I had no option but to find the culprit. You tell me who would have accepted my innocence? Nobody. I had to keep it quiet.'

He paused, nodding to himself once more in agreement.

'One of my colleagues is trying to sabotage my work, trying to make it look as though I am driving my patients insane, driving them to suicide.'

'Why didn't you go to the police for help?'

'Aha! It is always easy to be wise after the fact. But I suppose you are right. It was pride. The idea that someone was interfering with my work made me almost crazy with anger. Nobody attempts to ruin my career and gets away with it. I wanted the personal satisfaction of catching the man myself. So I went to Isaacs. He's got connections, that man. Well, he said he would keep it out of police hands, to give me a chance to catch him myself. He even helped investigate a little.' Brandsma shook his head. 'But I guess we weren't smart enough. Then when you became in-terested, I knew it was the end. I reckoned you would think it was me, the way I was trying to keep the police out of the way. And I knew that if you went to the police, my position would look bad. It was messy—very messy.'

Brandsma seated himself once more.

'So it's LSD, huh? And in ampoules of ergometrine. Very clever.'

Neal watched him with interest. If Brandsma was guilty, he was putting on quite a performance. No give-away ques-tions like 'Who else knows about this?' had been asked.

'There is of course the possibility that the whole thing has been a tragic mistake.'

'How's that?' Neal asked, startled.

'I suppose its possible that Argon Pharmaceuticals, who market the ergometrine, have been synthesizing LSD for some research purpose, and that the two drugs got mixed up somehow. But this is—how is the English expression? —a "long shot".'

Neal had not thought of that before. It was indeed poss-ible, but seemed unlikely. He watched Brandsma bury his face in his hands, sensing the moments ticking by.

Finally Brandsma drew himself to his feet.

'Here is what we will do. I'll phone one of the managers of Argon Pharmaceuticals—he is a personal friend of mine.

I will see whether they are doing any research into the psychopharmacology of LSD. If there is no such experiment in existence, I think we are left with only one alternative: a plot to sabotage my work, make me look bad. Then I think we should contact the police like I should have done ages ago.'

His reasoning seemed clear and above suspicion. Neal was becoming more confident of his innocence. He hoped it was not premature.

'If you will accompany me inside, I'll make the call. We can then take it further if necessary.'

Neal got up and followed Brandsma through the French windows into the luxurious but somewhat garishly decorated sitting-room. There was a Tretchikoff woman on one of the walls, her green face and purple lips setting the atmosphere. The carpets and the furniture were densely covered with wildly clashing flowery patterns. Brandsma went straight to the telephone in the corner, gesturing to Neal to take a seat.

Neal listened with half an ear as Brandsma spoke to the manager. His thoughts were elsewhere. If Professor Brandsma was not driving the women mad, then who was?

'Potter, it is bad news. Dr van Rensberg would know about any such research, and he flatly denies its existence. It is time to phone the police.'

Neal made sure that he could see the number Brandsma was dialling. It was 999. No colleague was being warned, no tracks were being covered.

When the phone call was finished, Brandsma replaced the receiver and turned round and faced the psychiatry registrar.

'I think you did the right thing, coming to me, I mean.' Brandsma was profoundly serious. 'After all, they are my patients. I am ultimately responsible.' He sank into the sofa next to Neal. 'I am meeting the police on the Obstetric Level in half an hour. Would you care to accompany me?'

'Thanks, but no. There is something I have to do,' Neal apologized. He had to find Jill.

Brandsma nodded. He got up, signalling it was time to leave.

'I'm sorry,' Neal said, not knowing what else to say.

'Not as sorry as the bastard who did this is going to be.' Brandsma punched his open hand. 'Wait till I get my hands on him . . .'

CHAPTER 25

Jill sped along the dirt road as fast as the van would take her. The road was not designed for the vehicle's ageing suspension, forcing her to cling to the steering-wheel and ride the van as if it was a wild horse. She headed in the direction of the highest ground. A vantage-point was needed.

Having found it, she swung the van to the edge of the road, piled out, scrambled on to the bonnet, and waited for the dust to settle. When it did, the high-rise buildings of Durban could be seen floating in the distance. Never before had they looked so welcoming, so like a sanctuary. The main coastal road could also be seen, and it looked as if she was heading in the right direction.

Back on the road, she tried to straighten out her thoughts. The final struggle had shaken her badly. The game was obviously being played in deadly earnest.

Keeping her eyes off the rear-view mirror was difficult. She half expected to see the nurse clinging to the side, but there was nothing but a cloud of dust.

When she reached the main road, she let the van slow down, let herself unwind. Her taut and tremulous muscles eased and, settling into the bucket seat of the van, she let the warm air streaming in through the broken window play with her hair. For a moment she almost forgot about the awful delivery room at the Umzimkulu Rehabilitation Unit.

Her mind must have gone blank, for when she next noticed, she was on the Marine Parade in Durban. She would first go home, she had decided, straighten herself out, and then make a few phone calls.

It was not long before she found herself driving into the underfloor parking area, only to find her parking bay occupied by a dusty-looking Ford.

Jill wondered for a moment who was visiting her, who had come from the country over dusty roads. Her brain must have had too much excitement because it took her longer to work out than she would have liked.

'Over dusty roads! Jesus!'

Jill accelerated into the garage and swung the van around the nearest concrete pillar with a screeching of tyres. Her heart felt as if it was about to burst up into her neck and she had to fight to stay in control of herself—and the vehicle.

Then the metal cross-bar dropped across the entrance, blocking the only exit from the garage. If ever Jill needed to make a rapid decision, it was now. Except that there weren't many options.

She stole a glance in her rear-view mirror. Someone was climbing into the Ford. Two of them!

There was only one chance left—but it was a slim one. From Jill's experience of having to lift the cross-bar, it was no mean obstruction. There was considerable doubt in her mind whether the old van would have the momentum to knock it aside.

The first man moved across the exit and stood confidently with his hands on his hips. When he got wind of Jill's intentions, he dived out of the way. Now the only thing separating Jill and the open road was the heavy cross-bar.

Jill strained to keep her eyes open, accelerated, and braced herself. With a deafening crash, she smashed into the cross-bar, and straight away knew that the van was far too light. The radiator caved in, the bonnet buckled and burst from its safety-catch and the windscreen shattered with the impact.

Jill herself was flung violently into the steering-wheel, bruising her ribcage. Then as the van shuddered backwards, leaving only a dent in the iron cross-bar, she bounced back in her bucket seat, her head rolling dangerously backwards.

She must have been momentarily dazed, because the next thing she knew, there was a squealing of tyres and the backfiring of a damaged exhaust. The rear-view mirror told her the rest. Driving towards her with more speed than seemed necessary was the truck. He was going to ram her!

Jill must have had her wits about her. She slammed the van into reverse, and with her foot pressed flat on the accelerator, jerked the van backwards and out of the way.

There was a second thunderous crash that echoed throughout the underground car park. This time the cross-bar gave way. The large Ford sliced through it with more than enough momentum to spare, deflected only slightly from its course.

It was a small deflection, but in the narrow exit it was enough. The Ford bounced off the kerb and through the thin wall with a shattering of glass and tearing of metal.

Jill took her cue. Ramming the gear into first, she screeched the van out of the broken exit and scraped it through the narrow gap between the back of the Ford and the kerb. There was no point waiting around.

Seconds later she was on the Marine Parade again and driving furiously, struggling to see through the shattered windscreen, nipping in and out of the traffic, and keeping an eye on the rear-view mirror. No dusty Ford. She breathed out. She just had to find help. Any more of this and she would cave in.

She decided she would go to John Peters—he would know what to do. He would be keen to help, she was sure of that. If anyone was concerned with justice in medicine, he was. If anyone was keen to stop Professor Brandsma and his plots to increase the fecundity of the Afrikaner, he was the man.

She had been to his house before and thankfully her topographical memory was good. He had held a cocktail party six months ago for the new registrars. This time her visit would be very different.

John Peters lived in a house on one of the rolling hills

outside the city. Sooner than she thought, she was parking the yellow van outside his house. Leaving the car, she ran up the driveway towards the red brick house. She needed help desperately, and Peters was just about the only doctor she could trust. She rang the doorbell and waited.

The house had a panoramic view of the harbour and coastline. Its eagle-eye perspective lent the city a peace that it ill deserved, she thought. When the details could be seen, it was a city in torment, a city that was in for a shock.

The door opened and Peters appeared, casually dressed in a light blue T-shirt and jeans.

'Hallo, Jill. What a surprise!'

'Hallo, Dr Peters . . .' She paused, not knowing how to continue.

'How can I help? You look a mess, if you don't mind my saying so.'

Jill glanced down at her crumpled and bloodied clothes, and nodded. 'I . . . want your advice. Can I come in?'

'Please.'

Peters held the door open and gestured for her to enter. Closing the door behind her, he led the way through the hall and into the lounge.

From the décor, it was obvious that he was unmarried. The soft feminine touch was missing, as were the disordered signs of young children. The hallway was panelled with dark wood like some eighteenth-century hunting lodge, and the lounge was stark and forbidding—modern wooden furniture on a sanded floor.

Jill shivered. She hoped his reception would not be so cold.

'You look a little shaken, Jill. Can I pour you a drink? I know it's early.'

'No, thank you.' Jill stood in the middle of the room.

Peters sank into one of the leather seats, and looked quizzically up at her. 'Well. How can I help?'

'I'm not too sure where to start, really,' Jill began, taking the cue from Peters and finding herself a chair. 'You're right about me being shaken—that's an understatement. When you hear what I have to tell you, I think you'll be shaken too. There is something terrible going on, and it's certainly too big for me to handle on my own . . .'

Peters raised his eyebrows. 'May I interrupt at this point. Why me? I mean, why have you come to me?'

'There is something I uncovered last night, and I have to tell someone urgently. If I don't, my life won't be worth beans. I had thought I could tell Neal Potter, my boyfriend, but I'm not sure any more—if he can be trusted, I mean. So I thought I should come to you . . .' Jill trailed off.

Peters nodded for her to continue.

'The other night Neal—he's a registrar in psychiatry— told me about a case of post-partum psychosis he had seen. It turned out to be induced by LSD, and not only that, records revealed other similar cases.

'We wondered whether Brandsma was driving the women mad, thereby stopping them from reproducing. You know how fixated Brandsma is about whites being outbred. It was a joke, really. At first. But the evidence seemed to stack up. It really looked like Brandsma was doing it. And on top of it, Neal seemed to be involved.'

Peters nodded sympathetically, urging her to continue.

'Well, I reckoned Brandsma was probably getting the psychotic women admitted to some place called the Umzimkulu Rehabilitation Unit—Neal told me that was where the cases ended up, and performing tubal ligations there. So I figured I had to pay it a visit.'

Peters pushed himself to his feet. He looked tense—his brow was deeply furrowed and his lips pursed.

'I don't know about you, but if I'm to take in any more of this story, I'm going to need a drink. And a stiff one. I think I can guess what is coming—more gross injustices against blacks. Jesus! Will it never end?' Peters shook his head angrily. 'Are you sure you won't join me? It will do you good . . .'

'Yes, I think I will.' Jill changed her mind. 'I probably need it more than you do. But you won't be able to guess what I found.'

Peters went to the cabinet in the corner of the room and removed a bottle and two glasses. He set them down on the mahogany coffee table in the middle of the room. Then, picking up the two glasses, he explained that he had to get some ice.

Jill sank back in the leather chair. The tension throughout her body began to ease. She was no longer on her own, she had help. John Peters would know what to do.

When he returned with the glasses filled with ice he proceeded to introduce a liberal helping of whisky into each. Handing Jill her drink, he sank back into the chair and stared at her. He raised his glass.

'To the solution of the problem, whatever it is.'

Jill nodded, and took a mouthful of the fiery liquid. It was strong. Almost spluttering, she continued the story.

'So I took it into my head to go and visit the Umzimkulu Rehabilitation Unit, thinking I might find some tubal ligation being performed. Instead, you won't believe what I found . . .'

Dr Peters no longer looked tense. 'Jill, I suggest you have another mouthful—it's relaxing stuff. And you still look pretty shaken. Are you sure you feel OK?'

Jill obediently gulped down another mouthful. Peters was right. With the release of tension, with the unburdening of the horrifying story, she suddenly felt quite weak, almost faint.

'I'm all right, thanks,' Jill reassured him. 'Let me finish before this stuff goes to my head, will you?'

She shook her head to clear it, but it only made the room rotate slowly about her. She stared hard at Peters to fix her world, and saw him smile back with encouragement.

'I got there in time, not for a tubal ligation, but for the delivery of a child. Now this might sound innocent enough. It didn't seem that one could accuse the Prof. of reducing their fertility after all.' Jill put her hand to her head. Things were going in and out of focus. 'Where was I? Oh yes. Well, it looked like Brandsma was not reducing the women's fertility, but increasing it. Except there was one hitch. The woman was black, and the child was as white as snow.'

'An albino?' Peters inquired.

'Uh-uh. The hair was pigmented, so the child couldn't have been . . . Ooh—I feel really woozy. What did you put in that drink?'

Peters got up from the chair and gazed down at Jill.

'Ketomine. What did you think?'

Jill squeezed her eyes closed and opened them again, hoping that she hadn't heard right. She managed a laugh, but it came out hollow.

'You're joking . . .'

'My dear little girl, I am not. You don't suppose that I would let you expose me, do you?'

The sudden gravity of her mistake clawed at her chest. She wanted to get up and run, to scream for help, to get away. But she only managed to get her head off the leather seat for a moment before it lolled back. The heat from her flushing skin spread over her body. Her eyes closed as the voice droned on.

'For years now frustrated couples have come to me, having endured years of infertility, willing to bankrupt themselves just to have their own child. As you might remember from your biology lessons, the desire for children is what drives the whole living world. With such a powerful desire, you can imagine the price a child was likely to fetch. I was sitting on a veritable goldmine! Good heavens, girl, some couples came to me saying that they would willingly give their houses, even a kidney, to have a child. Anyway, pretty soon I had the means to tap this goldmine, thanks to having a black infertility clinic to do some experimental work on. You see, the obvious way to solve the problem of women not having healthy wombs is to use someone else's. All you need is one of their ova, fertilize it with sperm from the husband, finally implanting the developing embryo in the healthy uterus of the surrogate mother.'

Jill watched as his leer rotated with the room. The shock of having made a mistake was now overtaken by an air of resignation—she felt tired, too tired to care. It was a difficult enough job just keeping her eyes open.

Worst of all she knew it was not a dream. Things were falling painfully into place. She remembered Peters's anger when she had seen the du Toits. It was no longer strange that a woman without a uterus had come to the clinic. She had come to rent a black womb.

Peters began strutting up and down, wagging his index finger to emphasize his points.

'I see from your crestfallen expression that you're a little disappointed in me. The defender of black rights turns his back on them, even uses them to perfect the technique of surrogate motherhood. Oh dear, you naïve little thing. Disillusionment is part of growing up, isn't it. Anyway, I was a pretty convincing liberal, don't you think?'

Peters paused, remembering something. 'Wait a minute, I can hear you say, it wouldn't work. The surrogate mother would reject the foreign embryo, and the pregnancy would abort. But you're wrong. Every natural fœtus is a foreign body that ought to be rejected by its mother. But somehow the fœtus is smart and blocks the synthesis of antibodies, preventing its rejection. And this system works in surrogate mothers too.'

He continued circling the coffee table, enjoying himself.

'But just when I had it sorted out, bloody bureaucracy gets in the way. First Dame Warnock led a bunch of moralistic Englishmen to outlaw commercial surrogacy—no woman could legally rent out her womb to any of those infertile couples to enable them to have a natural offspring. And then our own bloody government gets on the moral bandwagon.'

Peters stopped, turned to Jill and parodied: 'You can't buy and sell human beings, you know.' He shook his head, trying to control his anger. 'So the government makes it illegal to rent a womb. What was I to do? It was illegal for wives with uterine disease to find mothers to carry their children. It was illegal for me to start cashing in on that goldmine.'

He leant over to examine Jill, and nodded with satisfaction. 'So I was left with no choice. If they were not going to let me do it legally, I would have to do it without their sanctimonious consent. And I did it quite cleverly, don't you think?'

He waited briefly for her reply. There was none.

'Ignorant and obese black women were perfect. Nobody would guess they were pregnant, they were so fat. Not even they themselves knew. I could grow fœtuses under their own bloody noses and even they wouldn't know about it, let alone anyone else. The only problem I had to solve was how to get the use of their uteri for just nine months. I couldn't just go and put an advert in the newspaper. I'd end up in jail.

'And then it occurred to me. Get them into the backwater of some chronic psychiatric ward. Hell! Nobody would even be interested in their fate, let alone wonder whether they were pregnant. Nobody ever visits such psychiatric wards. And you know as well as I do that few relatives would have been able to afford the expensive bus ride. Even if they got there, what would they find? A fat and crazy woman—they would never guess that she was pregnant. If the woman was to say she was, who would believe a raving lunatic?

'The rest was easy,' Peters said gloatingly. He pulled up his chair and came to sit directly opposite Jill. She looked almost asleep.

'What I know about psychosis is dangerously little, but I do know about LSD—given enough of it, you go bananas. I'd even tried it in my youth. Make an ester, and hey presto! you have a depot preparation. And give a large enough dose, and the constant stream of LSD will keep the women mad. All we have to do then is to implant the fertilized ovum from one of my couples.'

Sunk deep into the chair, hardly able to move, Jill summoned enough energy to voice an objection.

'How can you justify depriving these women of their liberty—kidnapping them, and subjecting them to such torment?' she challenged weakly.

'Christ!' Peters propelled himself out of his chair and glared at her, his face reddening. 'You liberals make me sick. You go around with your wishy-washy ideas of respecting individual liberty, only to withdraw it when this serves the common good. You don't give anybody the liberty to refuse vaccinations, or to refuse treatment if they have open TB. But when I come along and tread on a little bit of liberty in aid of some general good, you get hysterical!'

He began pacing up and down again.

'Don't forget that the greatest liberal of all, John Stuart Mill, said that we should maximize the good of the greatest number. This means we have to balance the good and harm of each action. Now you tell me whether nine months of madness outweighs fifty years of barren misery?'

When he did not receive an answer, he prodded Jill's eyes open, making sure she was still listening.

'So, just like you, I'm infringing the liberty of others to decrease the overall misery of the world.' Peters smiled at this formulation. 'What a good boy am I.' His anger had been replaced with self-satisfaction.

'Which brings me, of course, to the question of what we are going to do with you.'

Peters gripped her thigh in a painful vice, forcing her eyes momentarily open again.

'Now I'm not going to let you interfere with my wonderful scheme. I'm afraid, my dear, that you are going to have to pay the price.'

Jill tried to keep her eyes open. They did not listen. She tried to concentrate on his words, but they were gone as soon as she had heard them, gone without comprehension. There was something about 'price'. What could he mean?

Peters left the room for a moment, and returned with a medical bag. He set it down on the coffee table, clicking it open.

'Now, isn't it very convenient that you have a family history of pananoid schizophrenia? You see, I know everything about my registrars. Who is going to believe such an extraordinary story when they also find that you are hallucinating, thought-disordered, and obviously sick. Well?'

He poked his finger at Jill's face, pretending she was capable of answering. He was enjoying himself.

'You give up? I'll tell you. Nobody. Nobody is going to believe the far-fetched paranoid ravings of your deranged mind.'

He pulled an ampoule of clear fluid from the medical bag on the coffee table, and straightened himself to tower over Jill. Breaking open the bag of a disposable syringe, and holding up the ampoule, he drew up the contents.

Jill was almost asleep. But not completely. The last thing she remembered was the sharp, stabbing pain in her thigh, a stimulus big enough to get her eyes open and to see Peters's distorted face leering at her.

And then she was out.

CHAPTER 26

Neal left Brandsma's house sure of one thing. He needed to find Jill.

Confronting the Professor had been useful—one suspect had been eliminated. However, he was now more confused than ever. He had absolutely no idea who was responsible.

Don't jump to conclusions, Neal cautioned himself. Brandsma might still be involved. I mean, what behaviour would be more calculated to allay suspicion than contacting the police? Perhaps the police are already aware of the scheme, and supporting it? What Afrikaans police unit would object to the promotion of white supremacy in South Africa?

Nevertheless, Neal's intuitions told him Professor Brandsma was innocent. The man might hate the idea of the Afrikaner tribe being swamped by a black wave washing over the shores of Southern Africa, but he was not prepared to adopt any means to prevent it.

He guided his Fiat towards Jill's flat, his thoughts now dominated by the girl with the straight blonde hair and the warm brown eyes. It was only two days since he had last seen her, and he missed her terribly. Unconsciously, his foot sank into the accelerator and the Fiat sped along the empty Saturday afternoon roads towards the sea front.

When he swung into her garage, he was hoping to see her white Mini waiting patiently for him. It wasn't there. All he saw was havoc.

Somehow he knew she had been responsible for the mangled cross-bar and battered wall, and prayed she was OK. Translated, that meant well. Perhaps he was being too keen to diagnose psychosis everywhere, but at the back of his mind there were genuine grounds for concern. There was her family history, she was at the right age for a first episode of schizophrenia, there was her sensitivity on the phone—even the way she was becoming ill resembled her aunt's illness. Perhaps these were not sufficient in themselves to cause concern, but together they added up. He didn't like the arithmetic.

He decided he would visit her parents—she might have spent the night there. His old telephone directory was retrieved from the back seat and scanned before the engine was fired back into life. With a squealing of old tyres on concrete, he headed out of the underfloor parking lot.

It was a short drive to Jacaranda, another well-to-do white suburb outside the city. Neal tried to control his anxieties, but it was difficult. He had the sort of personality that was bound to imagine the worst.

Perhaps to prepare myself in advance, he speculated to himself. He simply didn't like unpleasant surprises.

He found himself looking at the traffic on the road, thinking he might be lucky enough to spot her en route to or from her parents. He slowed his Fiat and studied the cars on the road, making himself giddy.

It was only because he was proceeding slowly that he was lucky enough to spot her. She was standing in the gulley next to her Mini, looking shaken and afraid, looking furtively around.

Without looking in his rear-view mirror, Neal swung the Fiat off the road beyond her car. In a few seconds he was sprinting towards her.

'Jill! Jill! Are you all right?'

She wasn't. She was a mess. Her clothes were dirty and torn, there was blood splattered on the front of her blouse, and she was visibly agitated and distressed. He wanted to give her a welcoming hug, but pulled himself up. Her expression of horror when she saw him knocked him back.

'Don't you come near me, Dr Potter. I know you're mixed up in all this.'

If Neal's worst fears needed any encouraging, then they weren't being disappointed. He groaned inwardly, suddenly feeling distressed and empty at the same time. But this was not a time to mourn—he needed to use all his psychiatric skills.

'Jill,' he said, trying to keep his voice calm and relaxed, 'what do you think I'm mixed up in?'

Jill stared at him suspiciously. 'Don't try a fast one on me. I know all about how you and Peters have been driving women mad, incarcerating them in Umzimkulu, and using them as surrogate mothers. So don't—'

Jill stopped mid-sentence, froze, and turned her head to listen.

'You won't get me, Peters, you bastard. I'm tougher than you think,' she shouted into empty space.

Neal tried not to let Jill's hallucinations distract him from digesting what she was saying. When he did, it hit him like sledgehammer in the solar plexus, making him breathless.

The black women were being used as surrogate mothers!

It was totally brilliant! But was it Peters who was behind it? It was hard to believe that the champion of black rights was so abusing them. Or had Jill's deranged mind simply conjured the idea out of a jumbled puzzle?

'. . . I warn you, Potter, don't try anything,' Jill finished.

'Jill, are you saying Peters is implanting embryos of white infertile couples into the post-partum psychotics?'

Jill nodded, and was about to reply when Neal interrupted.

'How do you know all this?'

'Because I was there. And now I'm a surrogate too . . . Oh God! Someone help me!'

Neal took her hand and gently pulled her round to face him. He knew psychiatrists were meant to challenge and not to collude with their patients' delusions, but he was running out of ideas.

'If they've got hold of you, Jill, then we need to get you to hospital quick, to the gynæcology ward for a Dilatation and Curettage.'

'I know. But why the sudden switch?' Jill's eyes narrowed.

'Listen, I know it looks like I'm involved. But I'm not, honest. I can explain.'

'Explain away, then, Dr Potter.' Jill retrieved her hand.

'Sure. But there's a place and a time. What you need now is a D and C to get rid of the implanted embryo. Then we can talk.'

Jill stared at him long and hard. It seemed to make sense.

'Right. But no monkey business.'

'No monkey business.'

He led her back to the Fiat, and quickly showed her in. He had to get there fast in case she changed her mind.

Once on the road, he could think. The idea that the obese black women were being used to provide wombs for white babies was very clever. But was it true? That was his problem. Was Jill upset over an awful discovery she had made at the Umzimkulu Rehabilitation Unit, or totally deluded? The difficulty in making judgements of insanity was that you had to be sure of where reality lay.

He glanced across at Jill. She was sitting rigidly in her seat like a wax model, not moving, not reacting, not seeing —not really there.

There was a third possibility. Perhaps Jill was telling the truth *and* was mad. Perhaps she had been caught discovering these facts, and given depot LSD in the hope that she might drive herself off Cliff Road. He would have to check this out as soon as they arrived. A blood sample would decide.

They continued in silence till they entered the city. Then Jill moved for the first time. There must have been something that caught her eye, for she started forwards, stared hard, and then ducked under the dashboard.

'What are you doing?'

'Can't you see?'

'See what, Jill?'

'Its one of them. Don't slow down, for God's sake. They're after me.'

Neal did not contradict her. Whatever the truth, one thing was beyond doubt: Jill needed admission. He concentrated on getting to Wellington as fast as possible. It was distressing to see the woman he loved so disturbed, so hopelessly lost. Any further delay was simply cruel.

They were there within another five minutes, Neal parking his Fiat on the road and hurriedly steering Jill inside the hospital towards the lift. After a brief wait, the lift doors opened and swallowed them up. When they passed Level 14, Jill started objecting, tugging her arm away from Neal.

'Hey! Where are we going? I told you I needed a D and C. We just passed the Gynæcology level.'

'I know, Jill. But we need to do some tests first, OK?' Neal lied.

Jill gave a vain but violent tug as Neal's grip tightened.

'I know what you're up to—don't think I'm stupid. You're taking me to the Psychiatric Unit, aren't you? You're one of them, I can tell. You're going to drive me mad like the others . . .'

'Jill, you aren't well at the moment, and you just have to trust me. Please. I would never do anything to hurt you . . .'

Jill started to scream and struggle with all her strength, kicking and punching. Neal closed his eyes against the assault, and shielded her from injuring herself on the walls. As a psychiatrist, he had quickly become accustomed to acting against a patient's will for the patient's own interests. This was no place to stop the habit.

With some difficulty, he managed to get as far as the entrance to the Psychiatric Unit. His finger stabbed at the alarm bell. Help was needed. In an instant nurses sprang from nowhere, restraining Jill, relieving Neal.

'She is hospital staff,' Neal addressed the huge bearded charge nurse coordinating the operations. 'Can we organize a private room?'

'Sure, Neal, no problem. Do you want the duty doctor notified?'

'No.' Neal thought for a moment. 'I think let's call in the consultant. I don't want any inexpert treatment. Who's on call?'

'Professor Evans.'

'Hmm. Well, the Prof. it'll have to be. Make him earn his living, huh?' Neal managed a smile.

'Any sedation, Neal?'

'No. That's not a good idea. I want the Prof. to see her first. We don't want to distort the clinical picture before we make a diagnosis. What I do want is a blood sample. Will you help?'

'Sure.'

The nurses dragged a now silently resisting Dr Jill Bates to a private room off the main corridor. She was soon inside and firmly made to sit on the bed. While the charge nurse and his fellow nursing sister held her still, Neal pulled twenty millilitres of blood from a vein. He had to pretend she was just one of his patients. Otherwise it would have been too painful.

'You'll be OK, my love,' he said to her, releasing the tourniquet.

Jill did not react. She just stared ahead, unseeing, now uncaring. Neal thanked the nursing staff, and ran for the Chemical Pathology Laboratory. He had to get away.

When he got to the laboratory, McKenzie was about to leave. He had the document in his hand ready to post.

'So? What happened?'

Neal suddenly remembered the visit. 'Oh yes. I'd almost forgotten. Brandsma is innocent, I reckon. In fact, he admitted that he had known about the cases all the time. Said he hadn't gone to the police because he thought that someone was sabotaging his work, and he wanted the satisfaction of catching the culprit himself. After I told him what we knew, he contacted the police. It all looked above board.'

'Hmm.' McKenzie thought for a moment. 'What did your built-in psychiatrically trained lie-detector tell you?'

'I think his nose is clean. But we should remain vigilant.'

'Agreed.'

'I know you want to leave,' Neal began, 'but this really won't take long, and it is really important.'

The urgency in Neal's voice conveyed itself to his friend. 'Hey. Is anything wrong?'

'In short, yes. Jill Bates is involved, and might have been given depot LSD.'

McKenzie frowned, but didn't push. Without a word, he grabbed one of the plain clotted tubes from Neal's sweaty hand and dropped it into the centrifuge. The machine was soon humming. They watched in silence.

After five minutes, McKenzie stopped the centrifuge and readied the mass spectrometer. He pipetted some of the clear yellow serum into a sample test-tube, feeding it into the machine. The command was then typed in. The fingerprint of the blood tube flashed up on the screen.

McKenzie then asked the machine whether the sample contained LSD decanoate. Neal waited, holding his breath. He could not bring himself to look.

Then the screen began to flash. McKenzie turned to face Neal.

'I'm sorry, Neal. It's negative. There is no LSD decanoate.'

CHAPTER 27

When Neal saw Professor Evans's expression, he knew the worst.

'Paranoid schizophrenia?'

Evans nodded sadly. 'Afraid so, Neal. I'm sorry.'

Neal could feel his backbone turn to jelly. He would have liked to have cried unashamedly. The news deserved that much. But he simply felt dead inside. And tired—tired beyond caring.

'It certainly looks like paranoid schizophrenia clinically,' Evans continued, breaking the uncomfortable silence. 'And if you combine that with her family history, the diagnosis is unavoidable.'

Neal didn't say anything.

'Now explain to me why you believe she might not be deluded. I would have thought I had trained my registrars better!'

'Oh, that,' Neal replied with little enthusiasm or hope. 'I know what you'll say: We're suffering from *folie à deux*.'

'Now you really have aroused my interest.' Evans sat down in his leather chair. 'Exactly what is this illusion you are sharing?'

Neal tried to rally some of his flagging energy, to put some life back into his voice. It wasn't easy. With little enthusiasm he recounted the story of the women getting depot LSD.

'Good God! That is extraordinary!' Evans exclaimed when Neal had finished. 'I see what you mean about my diagnosing you as paranoid.' He ran his hand through his hair.

'I reckon if you did not elaborate a paranoid theory, you really would be crazy,' Neal said paradoxically.

'Some paranoid theories can be true, you know. One of my patients was referred to me because he claimed his neighbours were spying on him. We had him committed, and in fact were thinking of treating him, when I suggested to my consultant—I was a registrar at that time—that I go and speak to the neighbours to collect more information.

'It turned out that the neighbours were surveillance buffs and were observing him through fibre-optic TV equipment. It's a lesson I have never forgotten. There is often more truth in a paranoid's view of the world than you think.'

Neal didn't reply. He was pleased that Evans had understood, and he was beginning to feel a little better. But things still looked pretty bad for Jill, pretty bad for himself and Jill. The prognosis for their happiness wasn't rosy.

'I suppose you've checked her blood levels?'

'Yes.'

'And?'

'Negative. Not a trace.'

'Hmm,' Evans said reflectively. 'Right. This story about the depot LSD is terrifying. Scary enough to make one wonder if there are other depot preparations of hallucinogenic compounds.'

While Evans twirled his walrus moustache in thought, Neal's spirits took a sharp upturn. Perhaps Jill did not have schizophrenia after all. A spine was returning to his flagging back, allowing him to straighten himself up.

'Is McKenzie around?' Evans asked.

'Not at the moment. He's off to lunch, I think.'

'OK. Here's what I'll do. I'll draw up a list of hallucinogenic compounds and ask McKenzie to test Jill's blood for them. Then we should contact the police.'

Neal shook his head. 'Going to the police won't work, Prof. What would we say? A girl with paranoid schizophrenia says that the women in the Umzimkulu Rehabilitation Unit are being used as surrogate mothers? I think they would simply call in the district psychiatrist and have us certified!'

Evans grinned. He knew Neal was right.

'Right. First things first. You get some rest—you deserve it. I'll sort this matter out.'

Neal nodded. But not in agreement. He had a personal

score to settle—no one could harm his girlfriend and get away with it. If Peters was to be stopped, he needed some more facts, facts that were waiting for him in the Umzimkulu Rehabilitation Unit. He had to show that the women there were pregnant. A fœtoscope would tell.

Neal headed for the lifts. If he went to the maternity wards, he ran the risk of running into an irate sister, the risk of the hospital administrator being called, and valuable time being lost.

He caught the lift for the ground floor. There were always one or two fœtoscopes kept in the Obstetric Outpatient Department. One could be picked up there. Once on the ground floor, Neal walked through to the admissions officer.

'Hi! Still no card game?'

'Bad news, my man. It's like cold turkey!'

Neal laughed. 'Do me another favour?'

'Sure.' The admissions officer leant back in his chair and smiled. 'Fire away.'

'I need the keys to the Obstetric Outpatients. And Pharmacy.'

The officer produced the keys and the register for Neal to sign.

'Remember, leave the morphine alone, OK?' the officer joked.

'Yessir.'

It was other drugs he was thinking of. If he was right about the attacks on his life, Peters knew all about him. And no doubt Jill would have told him he was dangerously close on his tail.

'If he's expecting me, I could be walking stupidly into a trap of terminal proportions,' Neal thought aloud. 'I had better be ready.'

Images of being drugged with sodium pentothal and buried alive, of being given a cardiac-arresting dose of potassium, flooded into his consciousness as he headed across Medical Casualty, and he shivered involuntarily. But he wasn't about to back down.

The Obstetric Department was just across from Medical

Casualty and Neal was soon inside, looking for the equipment room. It was at the end of the corridor, and Neal soon
had a fœtoscope tucked under his arm. He didn't forget to
pick up a few syringes and needles on his way out.

Next stop was the pharmacy. He needed some weapons.

The pharmacy was mercifully empty when he unlocked
and opened the door. No raised eyebrows would have to be
endured. No awkward explanations would have to be given.
Neal picked his way through the rows of shelved bottles
towards the anæsthetic cupboard. He knew he would find
the drugs he needed there. The cupboard wasn't difficult to
find, and he was soon scanning the rows of phials, finally
picking out a handful marked Pancuronium.

He promised himself he would only use the paralysing
agent in extreme emergencies.

His next stop was the psychiatry shelf where he retrieved
some bottles of sodium amytal.

'To slow 'em down,' he murmured, grinning.

Before leaving the pharmacy, he quickly loaded his
syringes, slipped on their protective caps and carefully
stowed them away in his pockets. On the way out he picked
up some test-tubes. There was the chance he could collect
more incriminating samples of blood. All prepared, he returned the keys to Reception.

At his Fiat he stashed the fœtoscope in his shoulder-bag
and slung it into the back of the car. Carefully avoiding
injecting himself with his arsenal, he climbed in, fired the
engine, and set off.

The journey was spent mainly on automatic pilot. Neal
had learnt this technique during his exhausting house job.
It was a useful substitute for sleep. Now it would have to
recharge his drooping powers of concentration. They would
be needed.

Sooner than expected, he was approaching the Umzimkulu Rehabilitation Unit from the dirt road below. He
pulled the Fiat into the long grass and stilled the engine.

What was needed was a tracing or two of a fœtal heart,
perhaps a sample of fœtal blood, maybe even a glimpse of

a secret nursery. And to get out alive. After a quick rehearsal of the plan of action, Neal shouldered the fœtoscope, took a deep breath, and climbed out.

The route up to the main building was becoming familiar. He was even beginning to feel blasé about it. But this feeling was short-lived. Lurking behind the shed, he looked into the right wing of the nearest block to see a nurse staring straight out at him. He pulled back, feeling his hands and feet grow cold. The whole business was starting all over again.

Neal waited a few minutes, then looked again. The coast was clear. Crouching over, he ran towards the central wing, having spotted a door at the end. The run was uneventful and, pressing himself against the wall, he took a rest, letting his breathing settle. There was no point being exhausted at the beginning of the search.

Listening with his ear to the door revealed nothing. He tried the door. It was open, and he slid inside. No one. He looked around, finding five doors leading off the end of the long corridor. He decided to start with the one marked Toilet.

He opened the door and bumped headlong into Nongoma, the medicine man, dressed this time in blue overalls.

As Neal tried to recover his balance, Nongoma's hand shot forward to pin Neal by the neck to the door. Then he felt the cold tip of steel pressing into his fifth left intercostal space.

'Now, white man, talk!'

Neal could only manage a choking sound. Nongoma wasn't in the mood for sympathizing—his grip tightened.

'What is going on here, white man?'

So it wasn't Nongoma behind it, after all. Was it Peters?

'Listen,' Neal gasped. 'I think Dr Peters is injecting black women with LSD, driving them mad, and then using their wombs to grow white children.' He paused for air. 'But I swear I have no part in it. I'm here to stop him.'

The grip weakened, slightly.

'How do you know this?'

'Air!' Neal croaked. 'I need air!'

'Talk, boy!' The grip tightened again.

'I ran laboratory tests on Selina Zondi's blood, and others in here; they were full of LSD. Thought you might be doing it, inadvertently, with mushrooms.'

Nongoma fixed Neal with his hypnotic stare, making him feel as if his life blood was being drained and analysed for veracity. Seconds ticked by while Nongoma communicated with Neal's guardian spirit.

Then he was released, Nongoma standing back to appraise him.

'Where do you come in?' Neal asked, massaging his bruised neck with relief, and taking in sharp gasps of air.

'Too many of my patients were going to the white man's hospital sane and coming out with the tokolosh in them. When it happened to my niece, I resolved to track down the evil white medicine that was doing this, and replace it with my own. The trail has led to 05 and 06, and now here.'

Nongoma paused, returning his hunting knife to the inside of his overalls.

'Hau! If what you say is true, there is much evil between these walls. I will kill this medicine man Peters.'

Neal raised his hand. 'No. We live by white man's law, like it or not. And if you do that, you will have to die too. We must get more evidence, and convict him in white courts.'

Nongoma shook his head. 'Hau! Such civility shown to evil men. I will never understand.'

'Listen, medicine man, I want to search this end of the asylum. Can you look elsewhere and see what you can find?'

Nongoma nodded.

'Good luck.' Neal managed a smile.

The witch doctor's face broke its impassive stare, and his white teeth flashed. Then he was gone.

Neal took a deep breath, focused his concentration, and after a brief look around the toilets, followed Nongoma into the corridor. There were four remaining doors. The first of these led into a sterile and empty operating theatre. There was nothing sinister to see. It was just an operating theatre.

The next door opened into a sluice room, as dirty as the theatre was clean, containing two large marble basins, metal buckets, scattered cleaning mops and rags, and a cleaning cupboard with cleaning fluids and powder.

It didn't look promising until he noticed there were bloodstains on the edge of the marble basin. He quickly scraped some blood off with his nail, storing it in his shirt pocket. If Jill was right, perhaps it could be analysed for fœtal blood groups.

As he left, he cast a cautionary glance down the corridor. There was no sign of any nurses. Neal tried the next door. It opened into what appeared to be the asylum's pharmacy. Rows of bottles crammed with tablets lined the loose wooden shelving on the walls. Neal scanned the labels for any unusual drug, any drug that might be used for obstetric cases.

But they were unremarkable. There were analgesics, antacids, neuroleptics, anti-diarrhœal agents, anti-convulsants, anæsthetic agents, tranquillizers, antiseptics, and other drugs one would find in the pharmacy of any psychiatric hospital.

At the end of the pharmacy was a fridge.

Probably contains thermolabile drugs like heparin, Neal thought. Still, I'd better have a look.

He reached for the fridge door and opened it. He wasn't ready for what he saw. He staggered back, catching a cry of horror in his throat. There were no drugs in the fridge, not that he could see.

Crammed into the top section of the fridge was a monstrous-looking baby—a huge forehead grafted on to a fish-like face, with webbed fingers and toes, and goitrous eyes glaring accusingly at him.

Neal started to breath heavily. The walls were closing in, and he was smothering. There was not enough air. Then he steadied himself on one of the shelves, closing his eyes and unshouldering the fœtoscope. He began to feel short of breath, even slightly dizzy. He was about to turn to get out of the confined area, when he froze. The hair on his back started to rise. He was being watched.

Neal spun round to look directly into the angry expression of the nurse he had met on his first visit.

'What the fuck do you think you're doing, man?' Nurse Davies barked, blocking the entrance.

It was clear to Neal that there was no way he was going to be able to bluff his way out. It was also clear that there was something dreadful going on, something the nurse was going to fight to keep from seeing the light of day.

The two men eyed one another as these truths sank in. There were not many options. If he was going to get out alive, he was going to have to act, and act fast.

Neal jammed his foot on to the lowest shelf of drugs. The shelving bracket acted as a fulcrum, forcing the far end of the shelf to shoot upwards, showering Davies with bottles of tablets from below. He staggered back, off balance.

Neal took two giant strides towards him and drove his foot with all his might into the nurse's groin. He knew it wasn't the Queensbury Rules, but this wasn't amateur boxing.

The nurse sucked in a huge draught of air, doubled over, and dropped to the floor.

Neal knew he could not leave him like that—he needed more time. Clasping his two hands as if they held a golf club, he swung them with all his might at the cowered head of the nurse.

There was a sharp crack as his knuckles made contact. The nurse's head jerked upwards, and he crashed back on to the shelves, finally crumpling under a further shower of bottles, unconscious.

Almost laughing with relief, Neal bounded over the prostrate figure, wrenched open the door, and headed down the corridor.

He ran as fast as he could. There was no doubt left in his mind, only certainty—the certainty that Jill was right, the certainty that he was no longer safe in the asylum.

He reached the large oak door without detection. Nearly home and dry. Then Neal opened the door and walked straight into Dr John Peters.

CHAPTER 28

'Good day, Dr Potter. What brings you here?'

Neal swallowed. For a moment his brain was numbed, shocked into a frustrating blankness. There was an intolerable silence while the two men stood awkwardly eyeing one another.

'I . . . was just visiting . . . some of our old patients,' Neal stammered, his brain suddenly functioning again.

Was there a chance that Peters wouldn't guess what he knew?

'And are they well?'

'The patients? Oh yes, I mean, no. Not really,' Neal faltered.

Silence again.

Neal was itching to get away, but he knew it would look odd if he did not ask some relevant questions.

'What brings you here?' he asked, keeping his voice as calm as possible.

Peters's eyes narrowed. 'I too have clinical responsibilities outside Wellington. I cover the gynæcological problems here.'

Another silence. Was he really going to get away?

'Well. Goodbye then.'

Then the door opened.

'Hawton,' Peters began, 'I was just saying to Dr Potter that I also have patients here. Did you show him around OK?'

Hawton frowned and looked perplexed. He shook his head. 'What do you mean—show him around?'

Neal felt an impulse to run, but something told him to suppress it.

'You should be more attentive to visitors, Hawton.' Then he turned to Neal. 'Well, don't let me keep you, Dr Potter.'

Neal could not understand it. He was going to get away with it. He watched Peters stand aside. Hardly trusting himself to walk, he started for the gate.

Then they all heard it—Davies's warning cry from down the corridor. There was an instant for a decision to be made. Neal knew the game was over, that he would have to make a break for it.

But Peters was quicker. His hand went for his pocket, and an instant later Neal found himself looking down the barrel of a handgun. It was over before he had taken another step.

'Nice try, Potter,' Peters began. 'But the game is up, as they say. Perhaps we should go inside and have a little talk. OK?'

He waved Neal back with his pistol, keeping his eyes trained on his every step. 'And don't try any funny stuff. I know how to use this thing.'

Neal could feel his face flush, the heat of despair sweeping over his body. If he tried to run for it, he knew he would be dead. Now Hawton was also brandishing a gun. There was nothing he could do.

Neal was led up the stairs and into the foyer, where he saw nursing officer Davies staggering up the corridor, grimacing as he walked. His face twisted into a sadistic smirk when he reached them.

'Let me dispose of him, Doc,' Davies suggested.

'In good time. What happened?'

'Bloody snoop found the reject. The parents haven't seen it, and I thought we needed to convince them they hadn't been double-crossed. Should've disposed of it, really . . .'

'Very sloppy,' Peters said evenly. 'Oh well, too late. We can't cry over spilt milk.'

Peters prodded his captive down the corridor towards his office, Davies and Hawton following behind. Each was thinking ahead. There could be no more charades: they all knew where they stood.

At the end of the corridor, Neal was shoved inside the office. It was sparsely furnished, a desk and chair under the window, a filing cabinet behind the door, a small bookshelf in the corner all on a cold concrete floor. Peters moved round and seated himself at his desk while the nurses prodded Neal into the centre of the room, standing on guard behind him.

'You've got yourself into a bit of a pickle, haven't you? Now what do you think we should do with you?' Peters began.

'You are not going to get away with this, you know,' Neal started.

'And why not? Who is going to stop me?'

'At least two other Wellington doctors know what is going on,' Neal replied.

'I suppose you are including your friend Jill Bates. As a raving lunatic, do you think she will make a reliable witness?' Peters sneered.

'Bastard!'

Neal flung himself forwards in a rage, wanting only to hurt the man standing before him, wanting only to see him scream in pain. For a moment, he forgot the nurses standing behind him.

The shattering pain of the butt of a gun on his scalp and the blindness that followed was an ample reminder. He stumbled forward, crashing to the floor. All he could hear was the gratified laugh of his assailant.

He was not sure whether he had lost consciousness or, if he had, how long he had been out, but the next thing he heard was Peters's strident voice haranguing him.

'By the time your colleagues realize what is going on, we will have tidied up the rest of the evidence. We have already done the abortions, the early Cæsarian sections, the patient transfers. It's not *our* safety you should be concerned with, it's *yours*.'

His head throbbed, and lifting his hand to it, he encountered the sticky and viscous feel of blood. In spite of this, he knew what was going on. He pushed himself to his feet,

but with the tensing of his abdominal muscles, the pressure
built up inside his skull. It made him gasp.

'I see Dr Potter is still with us.' Peters smiled at him
almost benevolently. 'Not for long, I hate to say.'

There was a pause in the conversation as Neal supported
himself on the desk, finally stepping shakily backwards to
confront Peters.

'Why the hell did you do it, Peters? I thought you were the
defender of human rights?' he challenged, playing for time.

'Ah, so that is what is bothering you, is it?' Peters leant
forward in his chair. 'You can't understand why the champion of black medical rights, the man who defends liberalism
in the heart of Afrikaner racist medicine, picks on black
women?'

Neal nodded, still trying to clear his head.

'My dear fellow, the question is back to front. You should
be asking why someone who picked on black women chose
to be a liberal. Well, it's obvious, isn't it? It's the perfect
cover. Who would suspect a liberal of perpetrating such a
scheme?'

Peters smiled with self-satisfaction.

'Anyway, I had to pick black women. Who else would
not be missed for nine months? Who else would not get a
second opinion? Who else could be stuck away in some
remote country asylum?'

'So you did it for greed, then?' Neal persisted.

Peters leant back in his chair.

'I see. The psychiatrist speaks out about human motiva-
tion, does he? No, let's just say it was a fair trade. The couples
got what they most wanted in the whole world—something
for which they would gladly have impoverished themselves.
And I was compensated for the risks I took.'

Peters pushed himself to his feet, wagging his finger
threateningly in Neal's face.

'Anyway, Potter, don't moralize to me. We're not talking
of destroying the lives of these women. It's just nine months
of haze that is at stake here, and compare that to the fifty
years of abject misery and torment of childlessness. Do you

think that it balances? Is your mathematics that poor? If you really were the humanist you claim to be you'd be standing where I am. Except that you are a lily-livered don't-step-on-anybody's-toes liberal, aren't you, Potter? You don't give a damn about reducing the sum total of human suffering, do you?'

'Stamping on individual rights can never be justified,' Neal retorted. 'Killing deformed babies can never be condoned . . .'

'Ah. You're referring to the monster in the fridge? My dear fellow, can you really expect me to give my clients deformed and imbecilic children? The occasional mutant is the price I have to pay for using LSD. It can be terratogenic, remember?'

Peters paused, suddenly growing serious. 'Enough of this. The lecture's over—you've wasted more than enough of my time already. Tie him up, Davies—there's a few things we still need to do. And Hawton, send those Durban City Council electricians away, will you?'

With that, Peters left the room. Davies set to his assignment with distasteful relish. He retrieved some strawy sisal rope from the bottom drawer of the filing cabinet, and secured Neal's hands behind his back so tightly that the sisal cut into the flesh. Hawton hung around with the shotgun as insurance.

Then Neal was shoved violently on to the floor, his face forced into the bare concrete by a bony knee. The rope was stretched to tie his ankles securely, and pulled taut to leave him rocking on his abdomen.

Then he was left alone.

CHAPTER 29

Neal was silent. He was straining to hear the muffled voices filtering through the door. There were phrases he missed, but one was unmistakable.

'. . . roll the Fiat off the cliff at Devil's Point.'

Neal froze. This was no game being played.

'God, I don't want to die,' he whispered.

Hearing himself mention his own death filled him with resolve.

'Not yet, not yet,' he reminded himself. 'Not if I have anything to do with it.'

It was time to think up a plan, to carry out the problem-solving techniques he taught to his patients.

'Define the problem: the sisal. List the solutions: cut it, or wriggle free. List the pros and cons: wriggling . . .'

Neal gave it a try, only to find himself more tightly constrained.

'. . . is going to amputate my arms. Therefore, cut it.'

Neal frowned, and started again.

'New problem: how to cut the sisal? List the solutions: I've no knife. But I've got glass test-tubes in my pocket . . .'

Neal knew what he had to do. Straining his feet forward as far as he could manage, he tried to bring his tied wrists sideways towards his pocket, while simultaneously leaning on to the opposite side to expose the pocket. It was hard work, his face furrowed with concentration, his eyes shut with pain as the sisal bit ever deeper and his back arched uncomfortably. When he felt he could endure it no longer, his head throbbing, his back aching, his wrists bleeding, he stretched his fingers to a test-tube and, gripping it with his index and middle finger, pulled it free. He let it drop on to the concrete floor at his side, allowing his taut muscles a welcome respite.

Then he began a rocking movement, slamming his face on to the unforgiving concrete, creeping inch by inch forwards, till his shoes were next to the test-tube. Moving on to the other side, he slammed both his feet on to the tube, smashing it to pieces.

The smashing glass was music to his ears. He was nearly done. The last task involved rolling on to his back, stretching the sisal tied between his legs and wrists tight, and sawing it over the glass splinters on the floor.

The most difficult thing was the positioning. Each time Neal felt he had it right, the elusive chip of glass jumped out from underneath the sisal. Sweat was now running freely off his face, stinging his eyes. His wrists and feet were numb from the constricted circulation, his arched back on fire, making him ache to take a rest, to give in.

It was the tension in the sisal that made the project feasible. The plan would otherwise have been doomed to failure. As it was, Neal was on the point of packing it in when the sisal snapped, throwing him flat on his back. He breathed a sigh of relief, and gave his searing muscles a break.

The sisal cut, Neal began to massage his hands and feet back to life. The blood returned to them with a fiery vengeance, making him grimace. If he was going to escape, he was going to have to get on with it.

Standing up was difficult. Walking almost impossible. He hobbled round on floppy feet to get the hang of it. As he was feeling more mobile, the sound of approaching footsteps wafted through the door.

Neal jumped across the room as quickly and quietly as his stiff limbs would permit. There was a chance he was not going to be disturbed. He wedged his foot against the door, keeping his hand on the key. He was going to wait for the last possible moment.

The footsteps approached the door and stopped. There was a pause. Neal held his breath. Then the doorknob turned. The second round had begun.

Neal thrust his shoulder into the door, slamming it closed, and twisted the key. Then without waiting to listen to the muffled cry of surprise, he threw himself across the room towards the window.

Neal could hear the door being rammed. Any delay was potentially fatal. He leapt on to the desk, opened the window, and dived out.

The earth flew up, banging into his outstretched hands and jarring his shoulders as he broke the fall. The impact took his breath away, breaking his rhythm.

Neal glanced about, getting his bearings. The western block was two hundred yards away. The fence was another hundred yards beyond that. Then there was the cover of trees.

He sprang to his feet, driving his legs like pistons into the earth, pumping his arms. It was a long time since he had run the two hundred metres, a long time since his knee injury. He prayed his knee would not seize up on him now. His life depended on it.

At one hundred yards he noticed his lungs go on fire. At one hundred and fifty yards his thighs began to deaden, crying out for more oxygen. Then he felt his knee click, pain shooting up his leg. His stride began to falter, his rhythm disintegrate. His head swayed from side to side with the effort, his shoulders hunched and tense. The pace dropped.

The last ten yards were the worst. Neal's muscles were no longer responding to his harsh commands, lactic acid was reaching cramping levels, oxygen debt was tearing him apart, and his knee was buckling.

The corner loomed. Neal made a last stagger. He was there. For a while, he stood with his hands on his knees, sucking in huge breaths of much-needed air, expelling the painful carbon dioxide. He was safe, for the moment.

His respiratory rate started to drop, and with it his pulse. He was recovering. It was time to think.

'Must keep my knee moving,' Neal panted. 'Don't want it seizing up altogether.'

Straightening up, he started walking around, surveying the scene as he mobilized his stiffening knee. Sloping away in front of him was the dry lawn leading to the perimeter fencing; beyond that, a clump of thorn trees and further shelter. He glanced round the corner. There was no sign of Peters and the nurses.

His rest was suddenly disrupted. In the distance he could make out the vicious barking of dogs.

Oh no!'

It was a body blow to his plans. There was no time to think, even less to act.

Neal knew the barking of dogs all too well. He had been on a safari trail in Kenya, and had watched wild dogs hunt. So he knew what they could do, knew they were no scavengers, knew the bark they made just before the kill.

He shuddered. The barking was becoming far too loud, far too vicious for his liking. He knew it would soon stop. That was when he would have to fight.

He cast his eyes frantically around for some stick, some object to keep them at a distance. Without one, he would be torn to shreds. There was nothing.

What am I going to do? Neal asked himself desperately. The dogs were getting closer, obviously heading in the right direction.

He spotted it in an alcove. A metal dustbin. Neal dashed towards it. He was not seeing a dustbin, but a shield. Whipping the lid off the bin, he fed his right arm through the handle. Then he barricaded himself into one of the corners with the bin protecting his legs. He was ready.

There were two of them, big, muscular, healthy, and very aggressive. They bounded round the corner almost falling over one another in their frenzy to reach their prey. Without hesitating they leapt forward into the alcove. The dogs were silent now, concentrating. Their fearful barking had done its job. Neal stiffened.

The leader bared his teeth, not in a snarl but in cold-blooded preparation. There was no emotion. This was the danger point. Then the dog lunged forward through the air, diving straight for Neal's neck veins.

Neal was ready. He slammed the lid into the dog's snout, deflecting it on to the wall. Then the other dog leapt at his throat.

Neal only had time to bring back his guard, preventing the dog from ripping out his jugulars. Then he struck. His left arm swung round in an arc, burying the syringe deep in the dog's neck, plunging the curare derivative into the tissues. The dog fell back, knocking over the bin.

He really needed more hands. As the first onslaught fell

back, the leader recovered, sprang, and sank its jaws deep into his thigh.

'Aagh!' Neal screamed with the pain.

He banged the lid down on the dog's head in a frantic attempt to smash himself free. But the dog only dug deeper into his raw flesh. The pain was incapacitating, expanding into his consciousness and expelling any rational thought.

Neal banged again, and again, only serving to bury the jaws deeper into his thigh. The dog held on, thrashing its head from side to side, tearing his flesh.

Neal could see the other bull-mastiff in his peripheral vision. It was staggering now, swaying, out of action, the syringe still deeply embedded in its neck. Seeing the syringe made him think clearly again.

He dug deep into his pocket for another. But the dog's bite was making it difficult to get it out. By now Neal was sweating from the pain, finding it difficult to exercise control on himself, finding it difficult to persist with the delicate task of extricating the syringe. But as the blood soaked its way up into Neal's pocket, spreading in a ring of fire, so it lubricated the movement of the syringe. It started to come, slowly at first. Then it was out.

Neal tremulously pulled off the cap and plunged the syringe deep into the neck of the animal. Almost at once, whether from the pain or from the local diffusion of the drug, the dog's bite began to weaken. Neal brought the lid down once more, smashing the dog free. It fell to the ground, staggered, and toppled over.

Neal surveyed the damage. His trouser leg was saturated with blood, blood which was now dripping into his shoes, spilling over and pooling round his foot. He dared not look any further.

'Jesus!' Neal tried to walk between the immmobilized dogs. 'Should have brought some morphine after all,' he hissed through clenched teeth.

'Cæsar! Alexander!' a faint voice called the dogs.

Neal grimaced. 'No more conquests for you guys, I'm afraid.'

He staggered on his two bad legs out of the alcove. Gritting his teeth, he stumbled down the gentle slope. It was difficult to see where he was heading, perspiration beading on his forehead and dropping down into his eyes as he ran. He did not care. The pain in his thigh was dominating all else.

The slope gave way suddenly to a ditch, making Neal stumble and fall, jarring his wound. Fresh blood gushed from the laceration, sinking into the dry earth. For a moment he considered reducing the blood supply with a tourniquet, but he needed the leg to work.

'Cæsar! Alexander! Here, boys!' The voice was still faint. They still didn't know Neal's whereabouts.

Neal pushed himself to his feet once more. 'Keep moving,' he urged.

In his blurred and swimming vision he made out the fence, willing it nearer. Yard by painful yard, the fence got closer, and beyond it the shelter of the trees. Keeping his body low, he stumbled down the slope almost on all fours, his hands stretched out in front of him, breaking his falls, acting as feet. Before he reached the shelter, he lifted his head to scan the fence.

There was a gap below it where the soil had been eroded. Neal spotted it and rolled. When he came to a stop, he was deep in the bush, out of sight, out of energy.

It was time to survey the damage. He tore his trousers to expose deep tooth-marks imprinted on his quadriceps, but that was not all. The dog had torn the muscle badly, leaving a jagged and loose flap. Neal closed his eyes. At least the bastard didn't get an artery, he consoled himself.

Stripping off his shirt, he loosely bandaged the leg. There was no point cutting off the blood supply, but it still made sense to secure the torn muscle. Then he listened for any sounds of pursuit. Apart from the noisy singing of crickets, there was nothing. A glance towards the asylum confirmed this. It was time to crawl on.

Neal did literally that. He eased himself on to his hands

and knees and moved forward in the tall grass beneath the trees, making for his Fiat. And freedom.

When he was in sight of the car, there was still no sign of the nurses. Neal double-checked.

If he had been thinking clearly, he would have realized that they would have put someone on guard at the car. But he was exhausted, his brain malfunctioning. Having the car so close was too much for him. He threw caution to the wind, pushed himself to his feet, and ran, the pain temporarily forgotten.

When he reached the car door, a figure stepped out from under the adjacent thorn tree. It was Peters. More importantly, there was a shotgun cradled in his arms.

'Nice try.' Peters smiled triumphantly. 'Too bad it didn't work.'

CHAPTER 30

Neal was too exhausted to try anything. He stood panting by the car, leaning against it. There was nothing he could do. No argument could be mounted against a shotgun.

With his back being prodded with the cold barrel, he was shoved and steered back towards the clinic. The pain in his leg, temporarily stayed by the hope of escape, returned with a vengeance. He limped and stumbled, his brain numbed into silence.

'Hey Doc, nice going,' Davies greeted them at the central block.

'Mmm.' Peters was impatient. 'I'm going to take him there myself. You guys cremate the aborted fœtuses—don't forget the monster in the fridge, and come and pick me up there. OK?'

Davies looked disappointed. 'Sure, Doc.'

Neal was led away. In spite of the difficulty, he knew it was time to start thinking again. If he didn't, he might not have another chance. It was not nice to be walking to one's coffin, and it was this thought that jarred his brain awake.

When they reached the Fiat, Peters prodded Neal towards the driver's seat.

'Right, punk, you drive. And any funny business, you get a gut full of lead. Understood?'

Neal nodded. He was pleased to be at the wheel. That way there was at least a chance. Not one to put any money on. But a chance.

He retrieved the keys from his back pocket before climbing in next to Peters and his gun. Getting the car to start was not easy. His tremulous hands made inserting the keys like threading a needle in a hurry. And there was the pain in his thigh, making a task out of depressing the clutch. After a struggle, he had the car on the dirt road.

'Where to?'

'Devil's Point, punk.'

'Don't know it.'

'Just drive, punk.' Peters jerked the shotgun into Neal's side, making him double over with pain, hitting his head on the steering-wheel.

Neal obeyed. If he had any more energy left, he would have to conserve it for more important matters.

They were soon winding their way up the coast. Neal glanced at the sea as they bounced along. It seemed indifferent to his plight, washing in an out of the alcoves, washing over the rocks, washing away any human trace. He shivered. Not if he could help it.

'Slow down, Potter,' Peters barked. 'There's a car up ahead. Let him go.'

Neal spotted a wisp of dust on the horizon.

Like hope burning out, he thought.

'Take the lower road,' Peters directed as they came to a fork.

Neal obeyed, his mind moving up a gear. From the height of the cliffs, he knew they were getting close. To Devil's Point. To the end. Unless he acted.

If it was going to happen, he would have to act soon. He inched the accelerator downwards, increasing the speed of the Fiat imperceptibly. Before long, the car was bouncing along over the dusty roads, taking the corners with a small skid, jolting its passengers in their seats.

From the terrain, Neal figured that Devil's Point was up ahead. The road snaked downwards, flirting with the edge of the cliff, and at one point curving sharply away from the edge at the bottom of a steep descent. It was Devil's Point, so named because it had claimed many lives, lives that were sent to the rocks below in speeding coffins of metal. Neal shuddered.

The next corner would have to be it.

Then they were there. Neal swung the steering-wheel violently as they entered the curve, then quickly depressed the door handle, driving himself against the door.

The car floated on the fine dust on the road, spinning round like a top, and flinging the two men to opposite sides of the car. Peters banged against the door, caught completely by surprise. When he re-orientated himself and looked across to vent his anger on the driver, all he could see was an empty seat. And a door standing wide on its hinges.

Neal had let the centrifugal force fling him out of the car, rolling himself up into a ball, and bouncing and scraping his way to a painful stop on the side of the road. If he had not already programmed his brain to get up and dive into the sugar cane, it might have taken all day to recover. As it was, within a few seconds he was uncoiling himself, pushing himself on to his feet, and stumbling towards the long, welcoming cane.

'Stop, Potter! Or you're a dead man!'

Neal did not falter. If he stopped, he was going to end up dead anyway.

There was a terrible cracking sound, making Neal shudder, lose balance, and fall, pain shooting up his spine. His face took the full impact of the fall, grating his flight to an agonizing end.

He lay there, waiting, knowing he was still alive, checking for the inevitable pool of blood that would drain his life away. There was none. He was still there.

Suddenly he rolled over. Had Peters missed? Had he merely fired in the air. He had to know.

Peters was walking slowly towards him, the sunlight behind him transforming him into a black apparition. His hand carried his gun pointed downwards. It was over.

Peters stumbled, recovered, and stood over him. He raised his gun slowly, as if to prolong the agony. Neal waited for the inevitable, but it seemed to take ages. He closed his eyes.

Then Peters fell over. Sticking from his back was a war-coated Zulu assegai.

'You all right, white man?' the reassuring voice of Nongoma sounded in his ear.

Neal twisted round to see Nongoma. There was no man in overalls, no man masquerading as a City Council electrician, no man seeking further evidence. Instead, he saw the silhouetted naked figure of Nongoma dressed in full headdress, holding a Zulu shield and assegai.

'Thank you, black man,' Neal replied in kind, intending it as a compliment. 'You saved my life.'

Nongoma nodded, looking across at the rustling of the sugar cane field.

'How did you get here?' Neal asked, not remembering the arrival of another car.

'I heard the talk of Devil's Point and went ahead. I've been waiting here for you.'

That wisp of dust on the road! It had been hope after all.

'Let me help you to the car,' Nongoma offered. 'It isn't over.'

He took Neal's arm and slung it over his shoulder, helping him back to his Fiat. The car was soon driven out of sight and parked next to an old blue van. In the van, old man Zondi sat waiting.

'Don't do it, medicine man. The nurses will be convicted.'

'No, white man. It is time for black justice.'

Neal could not have roused himself if he had tried. He waited passively, knowing what was to come. In what felt like no time at all, he watched a yellow van drive over the crest, saw a Zulu warrior uncoil his throwing arm to release an assegai, and gazed at the vehicle, its windscreen pierced, as it meandered inevitably down the road towards Devil's Point, then teetered on the edge, and toppled out of sight.

Justice had been done.

CHAPTER 31

Neal sat in the waiting-room, thinking about the last month. It had not been easy, because the doubt had always been there, like a cloud on the horizon. The depot might have precipitated a genuine schizophrenic illness. But now the cloud was dissipating. It was unlikely that Jill had schizophrenia—no schizophrenic illness could resolve this dramatically.

Jill had not been well for a month. The hallucinations had persisted, and so had the paranoid delusions. Evans had decided to knock her out, and had literally kept her unconscious with sodium amytal for a good deal of the time.

'Better to have a good sleep than a living nightmare,' he had said.

Now she had woken up, and Evans had pronounced her well. She could receive her first visitors, and Neal needed no encouragement. He hoped her bath would not take too long.

While he waited he remembered the tense moments when he had arrived back at the laboratory and asked McKenzie for the results on the full drug screen.

'I picked up an abnormal molecule in Jill's serum on electrophoresis.'

'And?'

McKenzie had gone over to the mass spectrometer and placed the sample in the receptacle. The spectral lines of the molecule had appeared on the monitoring screen. He then typed in the request for a molecular match.

'Here is the molecule of amphetamine. Look carefully,' he had said.

A new pattern of spectral lines had appeared on the screen, and the message NEGATIVE MATCH had flashed. McKenzie had ignored it.

'What we have to remember is that if she had amphetamines in her blood, it is likely to be in the depot form. In other words, amphetamine decanoate. Now look at the difference between the fingerprint of LSD and LSD decanoate.'

He had flashed up the two fingerprints on the screen, and pointed to the new spectral absorption bands generated by the combination with decanoate.

'Now just mentally add the same bands to the fingerprint of amphetamine. What do you get?'

'God! Its almost an exact match,' Neal had remarked.

'That's it. Close enough for us to conclude we are looking at amphetamine decanoate.'

Amphetamine decanoate. It had been music to his ears. They were the words he was thirsting to hear. They meant Jill did not have schizophrenia.

Neal fingered the newspaper on the coffee table. Waiting to see Jill made him feel like he was on his first date. He tried the newspaper for distraction.

On the front page was an article entitled 'MURDER CHARGES AGAINST WITCH DOCTOR DROPPED'. He read with interest:

The Durban Police have today decided not to press a charge of murder against Joseph Nongoma, resident witch doctor of Umfulosi Township.

Nongoma admitted to killing Dr John Peters, Consultant Obstetrician from Wellington Hospital, with the traditional Zulu assegai hurled into his back. In his defence, his lawyer, funded by the generosity of Wellington Hospital, had said Nongoma had reason to believe Dr Peters was about to murder Dr Neal Potter, also of Wellington Hospital, and that the intervention was the only course open to him. A sworn statement from Dr Potter confirms this story.

Earlier this month an inquest had delivered a verdict of accidental death in the case of two nurses, Frank Davies and David Hawton, who died at the same time when their van crashed over Devil's Point on the North Coast.

Dr Peters and his two nurses had been driving female black patients attending Wellington Hospital insane with LSD injections, and then using them as surrogate mothers for white fee-paying clientèle. Peters had made over 2 million rand in this enterprise. The white clientèle claim no knowledge of Peters's malevolent methods.

The Administrator of Wellington Hospital, Dr Michael Isaacs, issued a statement today condemning the behaviour of Dr Peters, and dissociating the hospital from such medical practice. 'Not since Dr Mengele performed his experiments in Auschwitz has the health of some been sacrificed for the well-being of others. Medicine in South Africa takes great pride in its good record of providing care to all races, and of never concentrating on the health of one population group at the expense of another . . .'

The door opened and the staff nurse announced 'She's ready!'

Neal put the newspaper down, and followed the nurse down the corridor of the private nursing home to the room at the end.

'All yours.' The nurse smiled knowingly.

All mine, Neal thought. I hope she's right.

He gently opened the door on a small room, lots of flowers, which were mostly his, and Jill sitting up in bed.

Without speaking, he went up to her and gave her a bear hug. He could feel her warm tears on his face, and knew it would be all right.

'Oh, Neal. God, I've missed you.'

'Me too.' He held her shoulders away from him and took a good look at her. 'Are you feeling OK?'

'Mmm. Now I am. Now I know the nightmare has ended.'

Neal grinned. 'You had us worried, you know.'

'You were concerned?' Jill raised her eyebrow quizzically.

Neal gently tweaked her cheek. 'Just a bit. Seriously for a moment, though, can I ask you something?'

'Sure.'

'How come you stopped trusting me *before* Peters gave you the injection? What had I done?'

Jill took a while to disentangle reality from illusion. 'Oh yes. You see, I overheard you talking to Brandsma in the corridor—something about keeping the work with the post-partum cases secret. And then I went to your room— sorry—and snooped around. I found some vials of LSD, and a cheque from Brandsma. I guess I added one and one and got three . . .'

Neal grinned, explaining. 'The vials of LSD were to standardize the mass spectrometer—we weren't too sure if it was LSD in the patient's blood. And the cheque was Brandsma's overdue payment for the assisting I'd done on his private patients . . .'

Jill put her finger on his lips.

'You don't have to explain. I trust you.'

Neal kissed the finger.

'I trust you've not lost your Impulse Disorder?' Jill said, smiling.

'Now hold on, Dr Bates. This is hardly what the doctor ordered.'

'Well, it's what this doctor ordered. Certainly the nurses know we're not to be disturbed.'

Neal's face creased into a grin. He was not about to complain.